D.A. Dwinell

Bloom Keepers

Guardian of the Stone
BOOK THREE

D.A. Dwinell
Bloom Keepers
This book is a work of fiction, and the events, incidents, locations,
and characters are products of the author's imagination or are used
fictitiously. Any resemblance to actual persons, living or dead,
businesses, companies, organizations, events, or locales is entirely
coincidental.
Copyright © 2022, D.A. Dwinell
Self-published

Scripture quotations taken from The Holy Bible, New
International Version® NIV®
Copyright © 1973 1978 1984 2011 by Biblica, Inc. TM
Used by permission. All rights reserved worldwide.

This book is dedicated to my parents and my brother. God truly blessed me when he put you in my life.

Special thanks go to Audrey, Mark, Deborah, and Bill.

One

I sat in the passenger's seat of my best friend Mechelle's new Ford Edge. I tried to pay attention as she chattered about people at her school and the few people we might get to see during our visit. From what I could make out of her school friends, it sounded like she did not have many. That bothered me. I realized I was only half listening to her. I was not being a good friend. As much as I tried to focus on what she was saying, my mind was on the stranger from the airport. His behavior was bizarre. It was apparent he had noticed the Bloom of Dreams. I thought for sure he might have followed us. However, it appeared he had left the gas station before we did.

I tried to get him out of my head as we pulled out of the station. Surely, it was just a coincidence we were heading in the same direction, and he just stopped at the same gas station as us. It was odd the taxi driver did not get gas and his passenger never got out of the car while they were there. *No way this is a coincidence!*

Mechelle finally took a break from her gabbing to catch her breath as we turned into the Versailles neighborhood. I hoped she would not bring up anything she had been saying because if there were an exam, I would have failed. She had lived in this neighborhood for the past five years. It was an expensive neighborhood with some interesting neighbors. The most interesting lived next door to her. Valerie was friendly but nosey. She seemed to pop up when least expected. Occasionally, she would get their mail out of the mailbox and bring it to them. *Odd.*

I looked back at Greg and noticed he was looking out the back window. I glanced back to see what had his attention. The taxi was behind us again. *What does he want?* We both watched him as we drove up to the guard gate. *Is he going to try and get in?* My body was tense. I could feel myself start to relax as the gate shut behind Mechelle's vehicle. The guard stopped the taxi. *That was close.* My curiosity about

1

the man was up. When he bumped into me at the airport, his attention was on the stone. I kept replaying the scene in my mind. I had not realized it, but the stone did not warn me of danger when he was near me, not even when he was following us.

As we pulled onto Mechelle's brick driveway, the memories of being at her home flooded into my mind. They were comforting. Mechelle's parents were always so nice and welcoming. Greg unloaded our bags, and we followed Mechelle into her home. As I crossed the threshold, the smell of cookies filled the air.

Peggy, Mechelle's mother, came down the hall and greeted us with a smile. She quickly pulled me to her. Her arms wrapped around me and squeezed me tightly like a young child would their favorite stuffed animal. She reacted just as my mother would if she had not seen me in a while. She said with a smile, "I've missed you, kid."

She had been like a second mother to me, and her hug made me feel loved. "I've missed you too," I said. She turned her attention to Greg. "I've heard a lot of amazing things about you, young man. You have been a blessing to Brooke. I'm looking forward to getting to know you better."

What sounded like a timer started chiming. "My cookies," she said as she walked briskly toward the kitchen.

"I'm going to show them to their rooms," Mechelle hollered in the kitchen's direction. She enthusiastically climbed the first few stairs before abruptly stopping and turning to address Greg. "Greg, leave your bag here. Your room is downstairs," she instructed.

Greg dropped his bag and followed us upstairs with my bag in hand. When we reached the top of the staircase, she took us to the room next to hers. It was where her grandmother slept when she was in town. "I figured I was staying in your room," I said confused.

"That's what I thought, but mom said we're adults now and we should have our own rooms," Mechelle informed me as she opened the curtains to let some light in. "There's some room in the closet if you want to hang anything up." She opened the bathroom door. "Here's your private bathroom, my lady," she said with a snicker.

I thanked her. I motioned for Greg to place my bag on the bed. Mechelle announced she was going to take Greg on a tour of the second floor. I tagged along. The house impressed him. Especially her parents' walk-through shower. He also commented on how Mechelle's room looked like it should be in a magazine. There was another guest room upstairs along with a second-floor den with its own pantry and mini-refrigerator.

We headed downstairs for the tour of the first floor. We had seen the living room, but she took us through it to the French doors leading to the back patio. There was a pool with a sunbathing area and a jacuzzi. Her property was on the water and had a wonderful view of the water fountain in the center of the lake. To the right was an outdoor kitchen. Patio furniture was throughout the foliage that surrounded the pool. She walked us into the house through a bathroom that had access to the patio. She explained this bathroom was to be used when we were wet from the pool. This was also the bathroom for the guest room. "This is your bathroom, but if we're using the pool, it'll need to be kept unlocked," she informed him. He had a nice room, as well.

Greg placed his bag on the bed and thanked her for the tour. Mechelle said, "We're not done yet." She took us to the kitchen, which opened to the den and dining room. Her mother greeted us again with warm chocolate chip cookies and a glass of milk.

After catching up with Peggy, we hung out in the pool for a while. It amazed Greg how beautiful everything looked. I was not sure he believed us when we said it was like this nearly all year. One would think Greg and Mechelle had known each other for years the way they talked to one another. Mechelle asked about Austin. I think she really liked him when she visited. Greg filled her in on what he had been doing and included his single status.

Greg and I had a moment alone when Mechelle went inside to get us some drinks. He swam over to me and wrapped his arms around me. "Thank you for bringing me with you." He placed his lips gently on mine.

The French door opened. It was Peggy and Mechelle, bringing out drinks and chips and guacamole. We both got out and enjoyed the snacks. We chatted with Peggy for a while about college life in Kentucky and how we enjoyed being there. She had inquired about my mother. I filled her in about my mother dating Lance.

We spent the rest of the evening hanging out by her pool, catching up. Many of my friends were still at college. Mechelle and I were blessed to have our schedules allow us to see each other for the weekend. Jim, Mechelle's father, made it home just in time for fish tacos on the patio. He and Greg really hit it off. Peggy had planned for us to go to a jewelry show the next day. Jim told us to have fun because he planned to take Greg to the range. Greg spent most of the evening talking to Jim about a multitude of outdoorsman types of things. While the girls chatted about fashion, makeup trends, and boys.

Before returning to the pool, we applied more sunscreen. The rays from the Florida sun had kissed my skin and left a nice tan. I was tired from being in the pool all day. I showered and headed to bed early. As I laid scrolling through social media on my phone, I tried not to think about the man from the airport. My gut told me I had not seen the last of him yet. I posted a few pictures I took during our swim. I heard a gentle knock on my door. "Come in," I instructed.

Mechelle popped her head through the doorway and said, "Want some company?" Not waiting for a response, she came in and shut the door, and plopped herself down next to me on the bed.

I sat up. We began talking like old times. No topic was off-limits, or at least that is how it used to be. I could not tell her my secret. For the safety of the Bloom of Dreams and its cradle, I could not disclose the powers it contained because of the danger it could put her in. She would not understand how I can move through walls, understand different languages I am not familiar with, or use telepathy to communicate. I could barely believe it myself. Thankfully, I could talk to the Bloom Keepers about it. Mechelle and I covered everything from the men in our lives to things we would like to do while we were in town.

Mechelle commented, "I like Greg. He's perfect for you. If you find a guy even half of what he is, I want to meet them." We both agreed Greg was a keeper. We were perfect for one another. She brought up Austin again. We talked about him and his family. She wanted to visit his farm. I told her about his mother being an amazing cook. Mechelle confided in me about some struggles she was having at school. She had not made many friends. We stayed up until midnight before Mechelle headed to bed.

My head hit the pillow, and my thoughts immediately returned to the stranger in the taxi. I knew I had never seen him before. Perhaps the Granaldi's hired him. *If they had not sent him, who did?* The more I thought about it, the more awake I became. *Stop it, Brooke! You need to go to sleep.* I closed my eyes, trying to think of complete blackness. Flashes of Anthony Granaldi III's kept creeping into my mind.

I prayed about it. My prayers continued until I dozed off.

Two

Running as fast as I could, I jumped from one roof to the next to escape Joseph. My heart was racing. It amazed me how easy it was to leap from one to the other. I turned back and noticed he was keeping up with me. I headed back to the ground floor. As I scaled down the building, I heard knocking. I stopped and looked around to locate the source of the noise. This allowed Joseph to get closer to me. I needed to escape. More knocking. I scanned the area again. *Where is that coming from?* It was getting louder.

"Brooke. It's Peggy. You need to wake up. Breakfast will be in twenty minutes," Peggy said, and knocked again. "Brooke?"

Realizing I was dreaming, I opened my eyes and remembered where I was. "I'm up. I'll be down shortly," I advised.

Ms. Carpenter was a sweetheart, but she hated people to be late for a meal. When I first met her, I did not understand why Mechelle had a different last name. Mechelle's full name was Mechelle Garcia Carpenter, but she goes by Garcia, and her mother goes by Carpenter. Mechelle explained it was a Hispanic thing. I sprang out of bed and could feel the tightness of the sunburn on my shoulders. A quick glance at my wardrobe. *What does one wear to a jewelry show?* My light blue sundress and some sandals seemed perfect. With my hair in a high ponytail, I skipped downstairs.

Greg was already at the table chatting with Mr. Carpenter. Mechelle was helping her mother with breakfast. They both greeted me before returning to their conversations. I made a cup of coffee before joining Greg and Jim at the table. I knew I was better off staying out of Peggy's way while she cooked.

For a moment, I listened to Jim and Greg discuss sports. My attention quickly moved to the aroma of the hazelnut coffee. It

5

caused my mouth to salivate just before I took my first sip. After a few sips, Mechelle and her mother began placing plates of French toast at each table setting. She adorned the toast with powdered sugar, kiwi, strawberries, and bananas. Once everyone was served, Mr. Carpenter said grace.

Fantastic was the best way to describe breakfast. Unlike my mother, Peggy was an amazing cook. I don't think she had ever made me anything I did not like.

Immediately following breakfast, the guys headed off to the range. We did the dishes before heading to the jewelry show. Peggy had me sit in the front seat. She asked, "Brooke, I noticed the setting for your grandmother's stone has changed. What made you decide to change it?"

Not knowing how to address the question, I looked at the stone. I answered, "I didn't know it when I received it, but it has two pendants. My grandmother preferred the other one. I like them both, but this one seems to work better for me." Impressed by my quick thinking and realizing I had not lied made me proud. The stone being in its cradle gave it greater power. I do not believe I have learned of all its powers yet, but I know the stone in its cradle could heal.

"Both settings are stunning," Peggy stated.

"Mom comes here every year to see if she can find a unique piece of jewelry. Dad gives her a budget and she must stick to it," Mechelle commented.

As soon as we parked in front of the jewelry show, Mrs. Carpenter departed the car. At the pace she was walking; she must be on a mission. Mechelle and I walked swiftly behind her. Her search began the minute we passed through the doors. Mechelle told her mom we were going to look around while she searched for her perfect piece. We looked for less expensive jewelry for ourselves. Mechelle tried on a lot of things. Her mother usually picked up something for her. We came across some sterling silver jewelry we both liked.

"Brooke, this choker would look great on you," she pointed to a necklace with a very tiny dragonfly. She knew I loved them. If I had not become the protector of the Bloom of Dreams and its cradle, this necklace would be mine. The Bloom of Dreams needed to always be with me, which meant I would not be wearing another necklace. It was not safe for me to remove it.

We wandered around for what felt like hours, taking turns keeping an eye on our location to Peggy. She had been spending a lot of time at one table, so we checked it out. The jeweler had his back to us while he assisted another customer.

Peggy asked, "Did you find anything you like?" Her eyes scanned the case in front of her.

Mechelle said as she looked down at the cabinet in front of her mother, "We found a few things. How about you?"

Her mother pointed at a ring in the case. It was a raw emerald set-in yellow gold. It was stunning.

"You've quite the unique necklace young lady," a deep voice announced.

Mechelle bumped me with her elbow. "He's talking to you, Brooke."

Moving my eyes toward the voice, I noticed a man's suit. My gaze shifted to his face. A face I thought I would never see again. It was the man in the taxi. I felt a lump in my throat. *Who was this man?* I tried to speak, but nothing came out. My heart started racing.

"I'm sorry for her rudeness. Brooke, this man just complimented your necklace," Mechelle said, sounding confused.

Realized they did not understand this was the man who followed us from the airport. "Thank you," I said awkwardly as I stared into his eyes.

With a smile, he asked, "Where did you acquire such a stone?"

The silence must have bothered Mechelle. She and Peggy kept looking at me, waiting for me to respond. I took a deep breath in and tried to calm myself down. In a matter-of-fact way, I announced, "It was my grandmothers." I grabbed the stone as if I was trying to conceal it from him.

"I've been looking for such a stone my entire life. In fact, many of my ancestors have tried and failed," he said in a hushed voice.

"Sir, I'm interested in the emerald ring," Peggy said, pointing to it in the case. He pulled the ring out of the display case and began showing it to her. As he spoke about the ring, he kept glancing at the Bloom of Dreams. The ring was a tad big, and he agreed to size the ring for her. He walked away for a minute to run her credit card.

Mechelle leaned over to me and asked quietly, "What's up with you? I've never seen you act so strange."

Not sure I should say anything. I leaned over and commented, "Not now. I'll explain later." As we waited for him to return, I realized the stone had never heated.

The man brought over her receipt and sized Peggy's finger. He wrote the date and time on the receipt for her to pick it up. His gaze moved to me. "Here's my card. If you're ever interested in selling the necklace, please call me," he requested.

Peggy and Mechelle walked away. Mechelle turned back and asked, "Are you coming, Brooke?"

"I'll be right there," I announced. I turned my attention to the jeweler. I leaned in close to him and asked, "Who are you and what do you know about this stone?" He seemed puzzled. Perhaps by my odd behavior to him.

"At one point, my family had a stone like that. One of my ancestors sold it to buy some land. The stone was in a setting like the one your stone is in, and you must admit the stone is very rare. We were told the man who bought it intended to have it reset because he did not think his wife would like the original setting."

I looked down at his card, Deonte Contee. His story checked out with what my ancestors wrote in the journal. I continued grilling, "What was the name of your ancestor that sold the stone?"

"Anan. They named my father after him," he said proudly.

Wanting to know more, I asked, "Why are you interested in the stone?" I wanted to know if he knew of its powers.

"Once Anan sold the stone, bad things started happening to our family. The land he purchased was not fertile. He had to sell the land and go back to shining shoes. Everyone believed it brought luck to my family. We need that luck now. My sister, Duhana, has been very sick, and there was a rumor that those that touched the stone were healed. I want the stone to heal my sister," he said, looking defeated.

I could not tell him the truth, "That sounds like crazy talk or something a gypsy would say? Can you imagine what could be done if this stone did have magical powers?" I hoped he believed me. "Look, the next time I'm in New York, I'll contact you. Write your home address on the card." I handed the card back to him. As soon as he returned it to me. I jotted off to find Mechelle and her mother.

"I see you didn't sell him the necklace," Peggy stated as she looked at my neck. "What do you think of this ring, Brooke?"

I looked at the delicate silver ring in the case. It was just my style and would complement the cradle perfectly. "It's gorgeous, but it's not your typical style," I informed her.

She had me try the ring on, and it was too big. She got the jeweler to agree to have it ready when her ring would be. We grabbed lunch before returning to Mechelle's home to meet back up with Greg.

Jim bragged about Greg's marksmanship and spent quite a while bragging about him. He seemed impressed with Greg. Apparently, Greg gave Jim some competition. Jim told him he should come back again. He wanted to take him to his hunting club. Greg began explaining about Austin being a better shot than him. This caught Mechelle's attention.

Greg loved the outdoors and had never seen the ocean. We changed into our swimsuits and headed to the beach. It was funny watching Greg hop across the hot sand to the water. It looked as if he had stepped on lava. He did all he could to keep his feet from lingering in one spot too long. The sand was warm but was not at the point of burning your feet as it does in the summer. We could not stay long because we had plans with my friend Maggie this evening. Greg seemed amazed at the size of the ocean. Unlike Mechelle's heated pool, the ocean was still a bit chilly for Mechelle and me. We decided to sunbathe.

Greg seemed to have no problem with the cool water. He seemed to enjoy himself. I decided to join Greg and left Mechelle who appeared to have fallen asleep. Just as I started to head down Greg was coming out of the water.

He did not seem to notice I was heading his way. The current had pushed him a little farther down the beach. I watched as he seemed to be trying to find us. When I was close enough, I hollered, "Are you lost?" Greg looked embarrassed. "If you're not paying attention the current will pull you down the shore. We're over there," I pointed toward Mechelle.

Greg hugged me and spun me around before kissing me, "That was so refreshing."

We walked back toward Mechelle holding hands. I watched as Greg looked for shells.

"I figured there would be shells all over the place. Where are they?"

I chuckled, "You are on the wrong coast for those. The east coast does not get many. If you go to the west coast of Florida, there are tons."

"I'm going to catch some rays. Do ya want to join me?"

"Not right now," I said as I admired his physique as he made his way to his towel.

Children's joyful noises could be heard between the crashing of the waves. These sounds brought fond memories. There are not many fond memories of my father, but we always enjoyed this beach. He and I would hold hands as the waves crashed and tried to pull me ashore. My father always kept me safe. Once we made it away from the breaking water, we would have the best days splashing at one another and hunting for shells and fish as we dove underwater. These memories made me miss Florida.

I watched the water kiss my feet as the waves crashed along the shore. We rarely went to the beach early in the year. I liked the water to be warmer, but I felt the ocean calling me in.

I edged forward, allowing the water to make its way up my body. I turned around and noticed Greg had sat up. He waved at me. God blessed me with him. Lost in my thoughts about him, I did not notice the large wave heading toward me. It knocked me over. *No need to go slow now.* I was soaked. I gradually waded away from the shore. My body was finally comfortable with the water temperature. *What the heck?* Something just touched my foot.

I went under the water to see what it was. A puffer fish was checking my foot out. I watched in amazement as it moved around me. The little guy was about six inches long with spiky skin. I desired to touch him, to see him puff up, but I did not want to stress him out. I just stared in amazement as he almost seemed attracted to me. He showed no fear of being in my presence.

Suddenly, I felt something grab my body and pulled to the surface. Shocked by the sight of Greg before me. Confused, I asked, "What's wrong?" I glanced over at Mechelle to see if she was okay. She was still lying on the beach.

As I tried to catch his breath, Greg snapped at me, "Brooke! You were underwater for a long time. I thought ya were drowning!"

I reached over and kissed him. "I'm fine, see." Spinning myself around to show him. "Forgive me. I didn't realize I was under for so long." *How long could it have been?* I said, "When I was watching a puffer fish, I never felt like I needed air. Time me!" I went under the water again. I started counting as well. *One, Two, Three,* ...

Greg pulled me up again, "What do ya mean by time' you? Ya could have drowned!"

His eyes scrunched up which told me he was concerned. "I'm fine. I have a theory. Please time how long I'm underwater." Greg still looked annoyed, but agreed to count.

I submerged myself again and started counting. *One, two, three,* ... *One hundred eighty-three.* I was tired of counting. I would let a little air out periodically. The puffer fish returned. I watched it again. I was not gasping for air or anything. Before returning to the surface, I grabbed Greg's toe. He nearly kicked me when he felt it. I resurfaced. Full of excitement, I said, "It looks like we found another benefit of the stone. I can stay underwater for a long time. You can just call me your little mermaid."

"I would like to call ya something, but mermaid was not what came to mind when I thought you were drowning. Ya scared me," he said, trying to look annoyed.

With a bat of my eyes and snuggle, I replied, "Please forgive me."

He reached over and gave me a kiss before pushing me under the water with him. We played around with each other for a bit. Greg captured me in his arms, which ended the horseplay. Without a word, we stared into the eyes of the other. We seemed to confess our love. Water ran from Greg's head down his face. He flung his head around, causing it to spray into the air. He looked so sexy. His skin glistened. I ran my hands up his arms to the back of his head. We lingered for a moment before gently kissing. I was lost in the moment. It was as if no one else existed.

With no notice, Greg lifted me up and tossed me. I could not help but laugh. We made our way back to the shore. Mechelle was sleeping peacefully when we returned to her. Greg and I looked at each other and knew what needed to be done. We started shaking the water off ourselves onto her. As soon as the water hit her, she jumped up in shock.

"It looks like she's up," I said, satisfied with myself. Mechelle grabbed a towel and dried herself. "We should head back to your house. We need to shower before dinner. Greg and I should pack also before the bonfire tonight. We are leaving early tomorrow to catch our flight."

I was nearly done packing, when Mechelle informed me, dinner would be ready in ten minutes. I took one last look around the room. My outfit for the next day was laid out next to my pajamas. My bathroom bag was still in the bathroom and would be packed in the morning.

Mechelle and I found Greg helping Peggy set the table. Jim was on the patio talking to what must be the next-door neighbor.

"Mechelle, inform your father that dinner's ready," Peggy said as she stirred the pot on the stove.

Mechelle opened the door. Upon seeing her, I could faintly hear him say, "I need to head to dinner. Have a good night."

We all sat down to eat a plate of Peggy's Paella. She frequently made this for me because she knew I loved it. We had a great conversation. I explained we had an Uber coming in the morning, so no one needed to miss church. They seemed grateful but seemed disappointed we were leaving so soon.

I had eaten too much. We did the dishes before heading to Maggie's house for a bonfire. We left the beauty of Wellington and moved into the rustic area of Loxahatchee. Mechelle pulled onto a dirt road. "It's amazing how different this area is. I could easily live here," Greg commented.

It amazed me how different areas of the same county could be. Loxahatchee was on the west side of Palm Beach County. The homes were typically on an acre or more. Many people had horses or other livestock. Maggie was not like most of our friends. She was into hunting and fishing. On rare occasions, her parents took us out on their airboat. I knew her for being a fantastic alligator hunter. Maggie stood about 5'7". She had long brown wavy hair with freckles that complimented her gorgeous face.

We arrived at sunset and headed to her backyard, which was where she would usually be found. Her yard had many interesting things that were not found at the usual home. There was an archery area with several targets set up, a dog obstacle course for Sage, their chocolate lab, and a small rope course. Her father was handy. He even built a stone firepit with a matching bench that went about halfway around the fire pit. The other side had patio chairs for seating. Maggie was in the middle of building the fire when we arrived. I ran over to her and said, "Howdy stranger."

Maggie jumped up and gave me a big hug. "Girl, I've missed you," she said before noticing Greg.

12

"I've missed you, too," I said before introducing her to him.

She reached over and gave him a hug, too. "Oh, before it gets dark, I want to show you my dad's latest handy work. You're going to love it." She grabbed my hand and pulled me toward the back of her property. She lived on five acres. I watched Greg as we passed the rope course. It was written all over his face he wanted to try it. The archery area was just past it. We continued heading toward the back of the property when we arrived at a small structure holding a target made of wood. Next to the target was a locked wooden box.

Maggie unlocked the box and pulled out a small hatchet. I looked over at Greg, who was smiling.

There were three rows of thick lines of paint on the ground: yellow, black, and red. She explained everyone not throwing needed to stay behind the red line. The thrower would start at the black line and should not cross the yellow line. She provided a brief explanation of the scoring. Maggie demonstrated how to throw the hatchet. She was just off a bit from hitting the center point. We each took turns chucking the hatchet at the target before the sun had completely set. Maggie and Greg did great. It was a bit of a competition between them. I was not doing bad and tried to keep up with them. Mechelle struggled to get the few points she got.

Maggie's sister, Kristian, brought out the makings for s'mores. She had a few of her friends over and they joined us by the fire. We enjoyed the evening, but it was getting late, and we needed to head back to Mechelle's house.

We headed down the dirt road toward her home. Mechelle expressed how much she enjoyed the weekend. She talked about how she missed hanging out in Palm Beach County. The more she talked, the more it reminded me she was not having the best time at her college. We turned onto a paved road. As we approached the next intersection, a Toyota Tundra ran the light and collided with a Kia Forte.

Mechelle stopped and put her hazards on. Greg and I jumped out of the car. I hollered to Mechelle, "Call 911!" Greg ran to the truck, and I ran to the Kia. The Kia driver appeared to be unconscious. Smoke started billowing out of the motor. I looked in the back seat and found two children. A boy about twelve and a young girl about eight. I tried to pull the door open, but it would not budge. A flicker of light from the hood caught my eye. Flames were now coming from the engine. I needed to save them. I thought about the risks of me doing what needed to be done. *Someone might see me.* I looked around and it was only us at the moment. I could not leave them here to die. My focus was on getting into the vehicle. I put my upper body through the door to unbuckle the children. I looked up at the girl and asked, "Can you walk?"

She nodded and asked, "Are you an angel?" She pointed to me. I looked at my body. It was going through the car door.

"Yes. I'll be back for you in a minute." I picked the boy up and pulled him through the door. The stone heated. I was sure it was healing the child. Greg and Mechelle were now standing behind me.

Greg informed me, "The other guys are okay." He reached out and took the boy.

I leaned back into the car. "Are you ready?" She nodded. I took her in my arms and pulled her out. Mechelle grabbed the girl without saying a word.

I turned back to the driver. She needed my help. I was about to enter the car again to get the children's mother when Greg grabbed my hand, "The neighbors are showing up. We need to get in another way."

I looked around, trying to figure out what to do as the fire became larger. I instructed, "Block me from their view."

He stood behind me to block the view of me and the car while I reached through the window and unlocked the car door. I pulled my arm back and said, "I got it." I backed up. Greg opened the car door and pulled the woman from the car. I reached over and took her pulse. She was alive. "Greg, put her by her children," I commanded.

"But Brooke, what if she doesn't make it?" he asked, sounding concerned.

"She will," I assured him. He placed her on the ground where I instructed. Mechelle put a jacket under her head. I placed my left hand on her head and my right hand on her arm. *Come on, heal this woman.* The stone heated. She moved.

The young girl crawled over to her mother and said, "Mommy, this angel's here to help us."

I looked over at Greg. He smiled. I turned to Mechelle, who seemed confused. Using telepathy, I told Greg, "We need to get out of here." I looked up at Mechelle and forcefully said, "Mechelle, I can't explain this right now, but you need to leave. Get in your car and start heading home."

14

Mechelle looked at me in shock. I looked up at her and mouthed, "We'll be fine. Just go."

Mechelle went to her car and turned it around to take another road home. The stone was still warm but was cooling down. I took my hands from the mother and placed a hand on each of the children. My hands and the stone were still warm. They must be hurt, too. I could hear the faint sound of sirens. The stone cooled down. I looked at the children and said, "Always remember, Jesus loves you. He's always watching over you." I pulled out my mirror. Greg grabbed my arm, and we vanished from the scene.

We arrived invisibly in the back of Mechelle's car. Using telepathy, I softly said, "Mechelle, pull the car over."

Mechelle looked frantically around the car before pulling over. She called out, "Brooke?" I brought us back visible. She saw us through the rear-view mirror. "I've lost my mind. You… You… went through a car. Brooke, the car door was not open… I watched a woman's wound heal right in front of me when you touched her. Please pinch me because this must be a dream," Mechelle said, seeming in shock.

I wish you were dreaming. Trying to calm her down, I said, "You've not lost your mind. I can explain. Take a deep breath in and slowly exhale." Mechelle did as I instructed. I turned to Greg and asked, "Greg, would you mind driving? She's in no condition to drive." I tried to figure out how to explain to her what had happened as Greg and Mechelle switched places.

"I need some directions," Greg advised us.

I pulled out my phone and set the mapping to bring us to Mechelle's house. I took a deep breath. *How should I tell her my biggest secret? Lord, I need some words.* I took another deep breath and said, "My grandmother and her family have been protectors of the Bloom of Dreams. When my grandmother passed, I became the new protector." I lifted the stone from my neck and continued, "This is the Bloom of Dreams. The power of it would be dangerous in the wrong hands. I can move through things. It also permits me to teleport, understand other languages, and… Well, I can become invisible," I explained.

Her face went from freaked out to confused to annoyed. She snapped, "Do you mean to tell me you can transport yourself, and now is the first time you are coming to see me?"

Yep. Annoyed is how I would describe her. I looked away. She was right; I should have come to see her. I would have if I had known she was not enjoying college. Knowing I was wrong, I replied, "Yes, you're right. I should have come to see you, but having the stone comes with a lot of risks. It's also a blessing. Some people want it and will do anything to get it. This puts me and those around me at risk. Especially those who know about its power." I grabbed her hands and looked her in the eye. "Mechelle, you can't tell anyone. Not even your parents," I informed her. I looked over at Greg, who seemed to listen. "You can't even tell anyone about the accident we witnessed. I can't be placed there. The little girl thinks an angel saved her. Perhaps everyone else will as well. I hope you understand," I pleaded.

"I understand. It's the whole magic thing that's hard to believe. I mean, I hear what you're saying, but it's like you're my little magical being," she said as she reached over and hugged me.

"I guess you're right. I'm still learning more every day. Hurting you was the last thing I wanted to do," I agreed. I told her what happened to me in the ocean.

When we got home, Greg headed to his room. I showered to get the smell of the smoke off. Mechelle and I hung out in her room discussing my life after Florida. I filled her in on my cousin Phillip and the Granaldis. Just as I was about to shut her door, Mechelle said, "You saved three people tonight, Brooke. I'm proud of you. Your grandmother was right to trust you with its powers."

I smiled, realizing she was right. As she closed my door, I heard Mechelle say, "You better visit more."

Three

Greg and I calculated the time we were to arrive home according to the flight and estimated travel time from the airport. Unfortunately, we missed church. Greg hung out for a while before returning home. I started my laundry before we sat down to discuss what I should do to help Deonte. We both agreed he could not have the necklace, but I should try to heal his sister. He headed home to let me finish my chores.

I helped Phyllis out and did my laundry. The backdoor could be heard opening and closing. *They must be home.* I was folding clothes when I heard them come in. I finished folding my clothes and went out to greet them, "Surprise!"

My mom pulled me in for a hug and said, "I missed you so much. How's Mechelle and her parents?"

I replied, "Everyone's good." I began telling her about all the things we did. She was a little shocked to hear about us hatchet-throwing with Maggie. She was not surprised by Maggie and Greg being so good at it. It surprised her I did well. She explained she was stuffed from lunch. Mom excused herself to change out of her church clothes.

I asked Phyllis, "Anything interesting happen while I was gone?"

"Yes. Thank you for reminding me," Phyllis announced. She went into the cabinet with the pots and pans and pulled out an envelope.

"That's a strange place to put your mail, Phyllis," I commented.

"It's a great place to hide something from your mother. She would never use a pan," she chuckled. "I didn't know what this was, so I thought it best if she was not aware of it." Phyllis handed me the letter.

17

It did not have a return address but on the front of the envelope was written URGENT. "I think I'll read this in my room," I said as I grabbed my laundry, placed the envelope between some clothes, and headed upstairs.

Curiosity about the contents of the envelope was making me want to race up the stairs. It felt a bit like a workout as I raced to my room with my laundry in hand. I plopped my clothes down on my bed not worrying if they would need to be refolded. I went to my door and looked out to ensure I did not see my mother before closing it. Nearly walking away, I returned to the door to lock it. I rummaged through my clothes to find the mystery letter.

I inspected the envelope postage. It came from Boone, North Carolina. I sat down wondering if I should open the letter. My heart was racing as I was overcome with curiosity and fear about what I was about to discover. *Just open it!*

Inside was a letter and a picture. The picture caught my eye. It appeared to be inside a fancy cabin. Unfolding the letter revealed what appeared to be a woman's handwriting.

Brooke,

Because of the sudden death of Lillie, I suspect you don't know who I am. Lillie was going to make you aware of my existence on your 18th birthday. I'm the daughter of Kelly Monette, your grandmother's cousin. We have been helping keep the family's most cherished item within the family. We, unlike some family members, believe it's safe with you.

My condolences on the loss of Lillie. She was an amazing woman and from what she has told me about you; you follow in her footsteps. Regretfully, I didn't think it was wise to attend her funeral for reasons I'm sure you understand. I hoped to meet you under different circumstances, but there's no time for polite introductions. We need to meet. I'm sure you know by now why I provided you the photograph. I'll wait for you to arrive, but remember this is an urgent matter.

Allison

I looked at the photograph again, but was startled by a knock on my door. My heart jumped to my throat. I shoved everything under the other chair's seat cushion and walked to the door to unlock it. I found my mother standing there.

18

"I want to let you know I'll be out of town this week. We've got a meeting in Vegas on Friday afternoon. Tim, my boss, has a brother with connections with the hotel we are staying at. I'll be hanging out some with him and his brother. Mary and Jerry moved to Boulder City a few years ago. I'm going to hang out with them some too," she said as she sat on the cushion with the letter hidden under it.

A sigh of relief. She did not notice the slight crinkle sound of the letter being squashed. My desire to speak with Allison was eating at me. Mom provided me with a few more details about the contract her boss was trying to get and how much she would miss visiting Mary and Jerry in the Florida Keys, but she was looking forward to having them show her around Vegas.

Mom was about to leave when I asked, "Did grandma have a cousin named Kelly with a daughter named Allison?"

Her face seemed surprised by my question. She replied, "Yes. I haven't thought about them in years. Your grandmother was very fond of Kelly. She would visit from time to time. I believe Allison was here maybe six months or so before your grandmother passed. I can't believe you remember them. Why do you ask?"

"Just curious. Being here has brought back some memories and there are photo albums in the library," I answered. She excused herself, asking not to be disturbed before dinner because she needed to pack and prepare for the meetings.

Perfect. I was certain Allison could be trusted. I called Phyllis and let her know about the letter before locking my door and focusing on the picture Allison sent me.

When I appeared invisible, there was no one in sight. I took in the splendor of the beautiful room. Multiple windows went from floor to ceiling just to the right of the fireplace. Dark brown leather sofas faced the hearth, providing a cozy feeling. The kitchen and dining room were just beyond the sitting area. Touches of red and brown accent added to the woodsy feeling. I glanced outside to take in the mountain view. Knowing Allison was expecting me, I made myself visible. As much as I wanted to see the rest of her home, I felt it would be rude. I hollered, "Allison, are you here?"

A voice from upstairs said, "Brooke, is that you?"

I looked toward the sound of the voice, "Yes, I'm by the fireplace."

A beautiful lady with light brown hair appeared on the balcony, "Wow, you've grown up to be a beautiful young lady." She disappeared. Soft footsteps could be heard coming down the stairs.

Allison came toward me, appearing to be excited to see me. Nothing had changed with the stone, so I knew I was not in danger. Before I knew it, she had me in her arms, giving me a tight hug.

She released her hold on me, "Look at you. You look so much like Lillie. More so than Sandra. I haven't seen you since your father died. "

Puzzled, I asked, "You saw me when he died?"

"Yes, my mother and I came to his funeral," she said, looking me over. "You were young and had a lot to deal with. I'm not surprised you don't remember."

We discussed the loss of my father and my grandmother. I discovered Allison was a very pleasant lady. I enjoyed spending time with her. She reminded me a little of Mechelle's mother.

Allison excused herself and returned a few minutes later with an envelope. She sat down with the envelope on her lap and began explaining, "My family has helped protect the stone long before Lillie had it. As a young child, I was being trained and didn't even know it. My parents had been preparing me from the time I could walk. I speak five languages, excelled in school, and even became a junior agent while in college. After graduation, I became an Intelligence Agent. Was it my dream to become an agent? No. I did it to have access to information that would aid our family in protecting the Bloom of Dreams. I also had Lillie help me solve a few cases. She was always so helpful. Don't get me wrong, I now love what I do to help our government. If they ever caught me doing something not related to one of my cases... Well, it could destroy me and possibly put me in prison, not to mention possibly exposing the secrets of the stone. This is a risk we all take to protect the Bloom of Dreams." She handed me the envelope.

I opened it and pulled the contents out. There were pictures of a woman and a few buildings.

"These were taken in Greece. The lady's name is Eleni Kostopoulos. She knows a little about the stone and wants it for herself. We're not sure how she came to be aware of its existence, but there's no doubt she knows of some of its powers. Eleni's a powerful woman with lots of money and connections. We believe she has kidnapped Kevin to get the journal."

I could feel my mouth hanging open in disbelief. I asked, "She has Kevin? How?"

"Kevin told me she had come around and was asking questions. He was worried about her and contacted me. We had been talking weekly to update one another on what we had found out. It has been over a week since we last spoke. I went to his apartment, and it was in shambles," she informed me.

My mind was racing with thoughts about Kevin and his parents. "Where do you think she has him? Are his parents, okay?"

"His parents are fine. Eleni has her own private jet. Her plane left JFK Airport four days ago, which was the last time his parents saw him. You can get in places without being detected. I need you to find him and we need to make sure she does not have the journal," she added.

"I know where the journal is and unless he disclosed its location, it's safe," I assured her.

She asked, with concern in her voice, "Why do you know where it is? Never mind. I guess it does not matter right now. Can you verify it's safe?"

"I'll be right back," I said before popping into the secret room at the Villa Dianella in Florence, Italy. It was still in the safe. I returned to Allison.

"It's safe," I said as I looked at the pictures of the buildings. "Do you suspect he's in one of these?"

"Yes. Eleni's plane flew into Athens. She owns all these properties. Each photo's address was written on the back," Allison said, pointing to the address on the back of one photograph. "You must be careful when dealing with Eleni. She has a lot of security and more than likely she'll be expecting you," she advised.

I thanked her for the information, collected the pictures, and informed her we will find him.

She looked at me puzzled, "We?"

I realized she knew nothing about the Bloom Keepers. The stone did not warn me of danger, which told me Allison was being truthful. I provided minimal details about how the group was created and informed her about Greg, Juliet, Jacob, and Phyllis. She was glad to hear Phyllis was helping me.

She handed me a phone and directed me, "Use this phone and only this phone to contact me. My number's programmed into it. I'll wait to hear from you. If I don't hear from you in a week, I'll come looking for you."

I nodded and returned to my room. I grabbed my phone and texted the group.

BROOKE: EMERGENCY! ASAP! Louisville Nature Center 2 pm?

JACOB: How about my house? My parents are out of town.

We all agreed to meet there. Greg and I drove over in case my mother looked for me. Phyllis could not come because she needed to help my mother pack. With pictures in hand, I was ready to fill in the group on our new mission. Jacob led us to his kitchen table, where Juliet was putting glasses of water.

Everyone was sitting comfortably. It occurred to me; that they did not know about the journal. I was most worried about how this was going to affect Greg. There was no way around it. They needed all the facts.

"Brooke, we're waiting for you," Juliet informed me.

I looked at the pictures in my hand and began, "My cousin Allison gave me these photographs. She and her family have been helping protect the stone for years. I found out about her this morning when I received a letter from her. She made me aware of the kidnapping of my cousin Kevin. He was taken because of his knowledge about the stone." I felt like something was stuck in my throat. "There's something I haven't told anyone." I looked at Greg, who sat up in his chair. "My cousin Kevin and his parents met with me about a journal my family has created for the Bloom of Dreams. Every person in my family tasked with protecting the stone has written about the powers they discovered. They also recorded any significant events that may have occurred. It includes the dates they were tasked with protecting it." I looked over at Greg, who was now looking away from me. "Thankfully, his parents are fine. We need to rescue him.," I insisted.

Juliet swallowed some water. "Where is he?"

"Allison believes he's in Greece," I said, looking at Greg, who seemed not to want to make eye contact with me.

With a little enthusiasm, Juliet asked, "Does this mean we're going to Greece?"

I nodded, "Jacob, can you find everything you can on an Eleni Kostopoulos and on these buildings?" I handed him the photographs.

Jacob nervously asked, "Sure. Um… How do you spell Kosto…? This Eleni's last name?" He looked over the photographs. "Never mind. Her name's on this photo. Oh, and I got addresses here, too," he announced.

Greg cleared his throat and said, "We need this information quickly if we're to find Kevin and keep this journal safe." He looked at me. "Where's the journal?"

"It's in the safe room at the villa," I replied.

"Let me grab my laptop. I should be able to supply information right away," Jacob replied as he pushed his chair back.

Juliet got up and grabbed a paper and pen from the kitchen counter. She flipped what appeared to be a grocery list over to display a clean piece of paper.

"Greg. Would you mind talking to me outside for a minute?" I asked.

We went out the back door. He appeared to be hurt. I apologized, "I'm sorry. I didn't tell you this before. I promised Kevin and his parents I wouldn't tell anyone. Phyllis doesn't even know. They explained to me the stone and the journal should never be together. The only reason I know where it is… Well… It's because someone was trying to get it and I hid it temporarily. See, I only got one peek at it and unless I've something to add to the journal, I'll never see it again."

My eyes also filled. I was choked up. Not having words for the love this man must feel for me, I hugged him tightly. Our embrace was like a turning point in our lives. At that moment, I knew how much I meant to him. The love I felt overwhelmed me. Greg revealed to me things I had never considered. I looked into his eyes. "You're right. It never occurred to me I should always tell someone. I'm sorry." A tear fell down my cheek, and he kissed it.

We walked back into the kitchen, hand in hand. Juliet shot me a look as if to say, "You okay". I gave her a nod to let her know everything was fine.

We spent the next few hours working with Jacob as he found information on the laptop. I needed to remember to thank Leonardo for the computer. With the information we discovered, we formulated a plan to find Kevin and Eleni. Kevin was our first priority. We needed to rescue him. After that, Eleni would be our target to bring down.

With everyone being in class tomorrow, we needed to start immediately. Fortunately, we all came prepared. Everyone agreed Jacob was not ready for a battle and needed to stay here. There were four storefronts and three of us. To cover more ground in a shorter amount of time, I was to drop Greg and Juliet off at a designated location. They would be invisible and would only collect information about the building. I would meet them back at the location I dropped them off at when I finished checking my building. Once completed, we would return to Jacob.

Just as we agreed we had a good plan, Jacob spoke up, "Um, Brooke. Will they stay invisible once you leave them?"

It never occurred to me the plan might not work. I responded, "Good question. I'm not sure. Let's test it." I grabbed Juliet by the hand, opened my mirror, and took her to my room. I asked her to keep looking in the full-length mirror until I returned. Neither of us saw our reflection when I left. I popped back to Jacob's house. Jacob and Greg seemed startled by my return. I took a gulp of my water and headed back to Juliet.

"Well," I said, wanting to know how it went.

She pointed to the mirror.

I could see her reflection. I grabbed her arm. "Plan B it is," I said, feeling disappointed.

Upon arriving in Jacob's kitchen, we informed them we would need to stay together. Greg and I knew we could go quite a distance at the same location and still be invisible. We decided to tackle each building together. It was nearly 11:00 pm in Athens. Unanimously, we agreed to start with the building closest to the airport because she would need to get him to a secret location quickly. We dressed in what was now known as our Bloom uniform or spy gear. Juliet and I put our hair back before putting on our gloves. Before the three of us headed to the building by the airport, I looked over the photographs and map of the locations Jacob provided.

Four

We appeared invisible just outside one of the many doors along the front of the old building. It appeared to be abandoned. There were no vehicles in the parking lot. The building had small glass panes for windows. There were quite a few broken windows. I looked at the building. It had six doors. "We should split up. Juliet, ya take the first two doors. I'll take the next two. Brooke, ya take the last two," Greg advised.

We nodded in agreement. Greg and Juliet started toward the building. "Wait. I'll contact you using telepathy to check in periodically to find out if you found anything or if you need help. Remember, just think about what you want me to hear, and I should hear it. I'll concentrate on listening to you. Don't speak it. We don't want anyone knowing we're there."

Rather than walk. I used my mirror to move to the far end of the building. I peeked in and saw what appeared to be a rundown storefront. I popped myself inside. It was eerily quiet. There was a door behind the far side of the counter. I confirmed I was wearing gloves before opening it. I took a deep breath and slowly exhaled. It did not seem to help calm my nerves. The door creaked a bit as it opened. It was extremely dark. I did not want to use my flashlight unless I was certain I was alone. I propped the door open and took a minute to allow my eyes to adjust to the light.

I wanted to know how the others were doing. Using telepathy, I asked, "Juliet, I'm checking in. How's it going?"

"Good. One window was unlocked, and I made it in," Juliet informed me.

I asked Greg, "Are you okay?"

He replied, "Yep, I'm going around back to see if I can get in that way. I can't get in through the front doors."

My eyes could see well enough to notice there was no one in the room. It appeared to be a storage area. There was another door in the back of the room. It should lead to the back of the building. Upon entering, I noticed a door in the corner of the room. It was closest to the front of the building. It was ajar. I peeked in and noticed it was a restroom. "Door number one done," I muttered in my head as I made a checkmark in the air with my index finger. I opened my mirror and pictured myself at the other door I was assigned.

I repeated the process and popped into the storefront. This one had a larger front room than the other unit. It, too, appeared to be abandoned. I went to the back room, and to my surprise, I found a small table with the laminate peeling off it. There were four metal chairs around it. The table had an ashtray on it. I took the ashtray to the front room to use the moonlight to get a better look at it. There were a couple of Marlboro filters. It surprised me to find an American brand. A quick peek in the bathroom revealed nothing.

I wanted to see how Greg was making out getting into the building. I asked him, "Are you in?"

"Yes, there was a small window above the door. I see nothing in here. I'm about to go to the unit next to Juliet's doors, "Greg stated.

I was feeling discouraged. I turned my focus to Juliet and asked, "Juliet, did you find anything?"

"Yes, can't talk. Come… Come quick," she spurted.

Without thinking, I popped in front of the building. *Which one?* I looked at both doors, confused. With concern, I asked, "Juliet! Which door?" She did not respond. A loud crash came from the door on the left. I looked through the window to see if I could see anything. I did not see her, so I teleported inside. The door to the backroom was behind the counter. I slid myself across the counter and made my way to the doorway. I looked inside and saw a man throwing punches into the air.

"I know you're here! Show yourself," the Greek man shouted.

Juliet took a broomstick and was using it as a weapon. She moved to the side of him and hit him firmly across the back. The man fell to the ground and pulled a gun from the back of his pants. With a swift move of her broomstick, Juliet knocked the gun out of his hand. She took the stick and hit him with full force behind the knees. He fell to the ground.

I could not help but smile at watching Juliet's amazing skills. She did not need my help.

He rolled over and started crawling in the direction the weapon had flung. She jumped on his back and pushed the broomstick against his neck. "Don't move another inch if you value your life," she demanded. I doubt he understood the words from her mouth, but he seemed to know he was defeated.

Not wanting the man to know there were two of us in the room. I used my telepathy to talk to Juliet, "Well done."

"Brooke? I think Kevin might be in that box," she motioned toward a wooden crate in the corner of the room. It looked to be about 3' x 3'. Using telepathy, I asked Kevin, "Are you in this box?" There was no answer. There were small holes along the top of the box. I looked in, but it was too dark to make anything out. I moved to the side of it to make sure I was not blocking the minimal light in the room from creeping into the box.

Jesus, please let him be okay. I poked my head inside the box and found Kevin curled up. I poked him and he stirred a bit. *Oh no, did they drug you?* Using telepathy, I said, "Juliet, I'll be back in a minute for you." I opened my mirror and held on to Kevin. *I hope this works.* I concentrated on my room at Villa Dianella. Thinking about us landing on the bed. I felt the mirror pull us in. We were flung on top of the bed, nearly missing it. Kevin stirred a bit. He appeared to fall back to sleep.

I returned to Juliet. She was still standing on the Greek man with the broom handle on the back of his neck. I grabbed her hand and took her with me to Kevin. She even brought the broom with her. "Stay with him. I'll be back," I instructed before leaving to get Greg.

I called out to him using telepathy, "Greg?"

"Where've ya been? I found some man. Well, actually, he found me because I'm visible," he said in a huff.

I felt horrible about leaving him. I assured him, "I can explain. Where are you?"

"I'm hiding behind the building in the bushes," he disclosed.

We reunited. I grabbed his arm, but he tried to pull away. "Where's Juliet?" he questioned.

Without a word, I took us to her. Greg looked over at Kevin, who was asleep on his stomach. He asked, "Is that Kevin?"

Juliet placed a wet washcloth on his head.

"Yes, I needed to find Isabella or Leonardo," I said as I rushed out the door. I felt like a crazy person running through the building. It was late. Only a few people were up. I knocked on the door to their room. When Leonardo opened it in his pajamas. I pushed myself past him and into his room. After a brief explanation of what had occurred, Leonardo grabbed a bag. He grabbed my arm, and I teleported us to my room.

Leonardo pulled a syringe out of his bag and injected its contents into Kevin. Juliet's face changed from concern to panic. In a concerned voice, she asked, "What are you doing?"

Kevin opened his eyes. Still groggy. He looked around the room. In a weak voice, he muttered, "Brooke."

"Yes," I said, moving through everyone to get to him. I sat on the bed next to him. "You're safe now, but you need to rest. Leonardo and Isabella are going to take care of you."

"Journal," he muttered.

"It's safe. Rest. I'll be back tomorrow. We can talk then," I said as I got up.

"I'll stay with him tonight," Leonardo assured me.

"I'm not sure when I'll return tomorrow, but I'll be back. Call me if you need me," I said, moving between Juliet and Greg to take them back to Jacob's house. We returned to him. He was still at the table working on his computer eating potato chips. Everyone took turns telling him how they assisted in locating him. We agreed it was a lot for one day. Our plan was to meet the next day to determine what our next step should be.

On the ride home, Greg said, "I understand why you had to leave me. I'm not mad."

I raised his hand, which was holding mine, and kissed it, "There was not a lot of time to think, and I knew Kevin needed medical attention. He was curled up in a small crate with just a few holes for air. It was so disturbing to see," I said as my mind filled with the image of him in the box. "I was so scared for him." He could have died. I started crying.

Greg released his hand from mine and put it on the steering wheel. He pulled the car over to the side of the road and unbuckled his seatbelt. He reached over and unbuckled mine. As only Greg could, he wrapped his arms around me and pulled me to him. He let me have a good cry on his shoulder. As I sobbed, I could feel him rub my back and my head to comfort me. When I started to calm down, I pulled my head up and looked into his eyes. "Thank you."

"Sweetie, ya are such a strong person. I admire ya strength, but even ya can't hold all these emotions in," he advised. He put a big grin on his face, "Me and my shoulder will always be here for ya." The comforting arms embraced me again.

Once I calmed down and we were moving again, I told him about Juliet, "Greg, you should have seen her. She was amazing with that broomstick. The man did not know what hit him." I chuckled. "I mean literally, he couldn't see her or the broomstick. He just knew he was being attacked by an invisible force." We both had a good laugh.

When I finally made it to bed, I spent the night tossing and turning as the image of Kevin kept sinking into my mind. I was finally able to sleep. I rarely remembered my dreams, but this one was so vivid. There was an image in front of me. I suspect it was an angel because of its incredible beauty. A halo of bright light surrounded the figure, and the air smelled of fragrant flowers. The angel pointed at the Bloom of Dreams and said, "God has blessed you with this. The Lord of Lords wants you to trust Him in all things." The angelic being vanished as quickly as it arrived.

I awoke and looked around my room. There was no being. I grabbed my bible to find what it said about the dreams. I was certain there was something in Matthew. *Found it!* Matthew 2:13. Joseph had an angel come to him. He told Joseph to take Mary as his wife and not to fear.

I had a hard time falling back to sleep as I thought about the message the Lord sent me. I felt as though I was on a cloud. One day, I would be with the Lord. I prayed and thanked God for the message before drifting off to sleep again.

Rather than work out, I headed to see Kevin at Villa Dianella before class. I stood in front of my mirror, trying to figure out where I should appear. I could not show up in my room because he might be changing or something. I remember the field behind the villa. I concentrated on it and stepped through my full-length mirror. There was a couple enjoying wine on the patio as I approached the building. I made my way to the check-in counter to look for Isabella. She was sorting through some mail.

"Brooke. It's so nice to see you," she said as she leaned over the counter. She whispered. "Kevin's in your room still. I'll let him know you're on your way to him."

I nodded and headed to the room. I was not paying much attention to the guests I passed. Kevin had my attention. I only had a short amount of time to see him. In case he was sleeping, I gently knocked on the door. As the door opened, I was relieved he was up.

He lunged at me with his arms open wide. Almost in tears, he uttered, "Thank you." He continued squeezing me.

"Kevin, perhaps we should step into your room and talk. I don't have a lot of time," I encouraged him.

He broke his grip on me. "Of course. Come in."

I noticed him scan the hallway before closing the door. "I can't thank you enough for saving me. That was a terrifying experience. Fortunately, they seemed to drug me when I wasn't being grilled by them."

I could see on his face he appeared changed by the event. My heart ached for him. He usually appears self-confident, but today he was timid and scared. "I can't imagine what you have been through. I'm sorry we could not get to you sooner. Thank God, you're safe. You had me scared to death last night," I informed him.

"Being in that box felt like I was being buried alive. I've no idea how long they had me there," he said with tears in his eyes.

There was no way I would ever understand what he was going through at this moment. I just hugged him and felt the tears stream down my face as he cried. Knowing he should not be alone, I asked, "Are your parents safe?"

"Yes. They were not in the building when they came for us. I'm sure they went to one of our safe houses," he informed me.

Not wanting to pry, but needing answers, I said, "Leonardo and Isabella will take great care of you. You can stay here as long as you need. If you don't think it's safe in this room, they'll get you to a secure location. I must ask what you know about what happened to you?"

"Just before my flight landed in New York City, a male flight attendant told me a supervisor from the airline wanted to speak with me after the flight. He asked me to be the last to exit the plane," he paused and looked down for a moment and then around the room for a few seconds before continuing. "Once the last person passed my aisle, I got up to retrieve my suitcase. I turned toward the front of the plane and headed toward the exit door when someone from behind me covered my mouth with a cloth. The next thing I knew, I was tied to a chair being questioned and beaten."

That explained the bruises all over him. I asked, "Did they ask about the stone?"

"Yes. They also knew about the journal." He shook his head. "For the life of me, I can't figure out how they knew about it. I didn't think anyone outside the family knew of its existence."

Kevin appeared to be afraid, but I pressed on, "Did you tell them anything?"

"They knew Lillie died, but they didn't say anything about you. A couple of men were questioning me. They had strong accents. Greek, I think. They also had bad breath," he said as he adjusted his position on the bed. "I never saw anyone because they had me blindfolded, but I heard someone in heels walking around. She didn't speak loud enough for me to make out what she was saying. It sounded like she was talking with one of the men behind me. They kept demanding the journal and threatened my family. I denied knowing anything. After what felt like days of questioning and torture, they drugged me. I was put in what felt like a small wooden box. I've no idea what they got out of me after that. I just remember images of them beating me."

I felt a lump in my throat listening to his story. "I believe the woman was Eleni Kostopoulos. Can you try to figure out where your parents may have gone so I can check up on them?"

"Yes. I would appreciate that. I'm sure they're still looking for them. There are a few ways for me to locate them. They'll stay in hiding until they hear from me. I'll have the information for you the next time I see you. You should know, when something like this happens, we'll contact either you or Alison if we can't locate each other," he informed me.

"I need to go, but if you think of anything that could help, let me know. Oh, I nearly forgot. I'll call Allison to let her know you are okay," I said. I hugged him before heading back to my home. The time caught my attention. If I did not rush, I would be late for class.

I grabbed my backpack, and the phone Allison gave me on my way out the door. Before exiting my driveway, I called Allison to inform her about Kevin's rescue as I drove to class.

"Thank God you got to him in time. I've been in contact with his parents. They're fine. You shouldn't draw any attention to them," she suggested.

I understood what she was saying, but knew it was not the best thing for Kevin. Kevin seems a bit lost right now, I advised her. I

31

think he would prefer to be with his family after all the trauma he just went through."

I heard Allison take a deep breath before she responded, "Perhaps you're right. The journal shouldn't be anywhere near him and his parents until Eleni Kostopoulos is dealt with."

"I've got to get into class before I'm late. We'll talk soon. Bye," I said abruptly as I slammed my car into park. I leaped from my vehicle and raced to my class. I nearly collided with the door frame as I turned too fast through the doorway. To my surprise, the professor was not there yet. I sat and tried to catch my breath.

"You're cutting it close," the person sitting next to me muttered.

I looked over at him. He was an attractive Hispanic man with a friendly smile. "Yeah, I feel like I'm moving in slow and reverse today."

He leaned toward me with his arm outstretched. "I'm Mark."

The instructor walked in crying out, "Quiet down, everyone! We need to get started."

I leaned over toward Mark. "I'm Brooke."

I spent the entire class half listening to her discussion. My mind was on Eleni Kostopoulos. *How did she find out about the journal? Surely, she knows I have the necklace.* I had run a variety of different scenarios in my head about what she might have known. It was giving me a headache trying to figure out how she found out what she already knew. The truth was, we really knew nothing about her.

The class was dismissed. Mark turned to me, "I saw on the syllabus we have a project. We'll need a partner for coming up. Would you want to be partners?"

"Perhaps. Sorry, I need to get going," I said as I made my way to the door. I could only describe my actions as being rude. As I raced to my next class, I heard someone yelling Deonte. This reminded me of Deonte Contee. I decided it was a perfect time to help him. I needed something to take my mind off things until I could figure out what to do next with Eleni.

Five

I came home from class and found Phyllis in the kitchen making meatloaf. With Mom leaving in the morning for another trip, I figured the Bloom Keepers could meet at my house. "Phyllis, do you mind if we have a Bloom Keeper's meeting here tomorrow night during dinner?"

She walked over to the sink to wash her hands. "That's fine. What do you want to eat?"

"Something simple. I don't want you going to a lot of trouble. We could even pick up something," I said as I grabbed a slice of raw potato from the cutting board and salted it.

She looked at me and rolled her eyes. "I will never understand why you like raw potatoes. How about shrimp and grits?"

"Yum. I'm not sure they'll eat grits and mom would hate to miss that dinner. How about some chicken and dumplings?" I said, rolling my eyes up in hopes she would say yes before making eye contact again.

She leaned over and kissed me on the cheek. "Anything for you."

I leaned over and snuck another piece of potato, knowing she saw me. "Well, I need to study." I headed up to the library. I plopped my backpack on the desk and texted everyone.

> **BROOKE:** We need to figure out our next step with EK. 6:30 dinner at my house tomorrow.

I grabbed the business card I received from Deonte Contee. I was able to pull up his home online. He lived in Smithtown, New York. Black shutters were on the windows of the white home. If Deonte was not home yet, he should be soon. I showed up invisible.

33

The home was a split level. There were no windows on the lower level of the home to see into his home. I put my head through the front door. The house was silent.

Duhana needed to be healed without either of them knowing. I looked around, trying to figure out where to begin my search. *Deonte, where would you keep Duhana's address?* I searched the kitchen for an address book but did not locate one. As I closed a drawer, a black poodle walked in on me. He seemed to know I was there, but just looked in my direction with his head tilted. "Aren't you sweet," I said, hoping he was. I moved throughout the house, searching. When I came to his office, I was hoping I would stumble upon something with her information. After going through nearly every inch of the room, I had not turned up a single clue. He must keep everything on his computer.

I heard, "Ozzy! Come here Ozzy!" Followed by a door shutting.

Ozzy was not moving. He just kept staring at me, moving his head back and forth. I motioned with my hand and whispered, "Go." Feeling stupid. *Why are you motioning to him, Brooke? He can't see you.*

Deonte appeared in the doorway. "Ozzy, what're you doing in here? I've been calling you." Ozzy did not move. Deonte leaned against the door frame and watched Ozzy as he stared in my direction. Speaking louder, "Ozzy." Ozzy turned his head and looked for a moment before returning his gaze back to me.

I tried to move but was worried about the wood floors creaking. I pulled out my mirror and teleported myself behind a bush in front of his home. Knowing I needed to get the address from him, I made myself visible before walking to the front door and ringing the bell.

Deonte opened the door. "It's you," he said, staring at me. There was no change in the stone.

I asked, "May I come in?"

He moved back and opened the door wider. "Yes, please come in. I can't believe you are here."

Ozzy started barking at me. "I don't know what has gotten into him today. He has been acting weird since I got home. This is not like him. Now Ozzy, be nice."

I knelt and put my hand out for Ozzy to smell. He turned his head at me, and in a timid way, approached me. He seemed to like me. I reached out and gently ran my hand down his back, feeling his soft curls. He jumped up toward my face and licked me. After a minute of enjoying his welcome, I focused on Deonte. "He's sweet.

I'm here about Duhana. I really don't know how I can help you with your sister, but I trust God has a reason for bringing us together."

"I'm not sure you can either," he said, looking sad. "Duhana's very ill from cancer. They say she'll only live a few more months. Would you mind going with me to visit her?"

I agreed, and he drove us to the hospital. We arrived at her door, room 313. Deonte went in first. After a brief time, he motioned for me to join them. Her room smelled of cleaning products and was chilly. Duhana was a beautiful woman. The cancer seemed to take a toll on her. I stood there listening as Deonte explained who I was. She moved her head in my direction and peeked up at me.

It occurred to me that if I touched her, they would both know the power of the stone. I leaned over and grabbed her hand, making sure the stone was just dangling above her and not touching my skin. I asked, "Duhana, do you mind if I pray for you?" Deonte smiled, and Duhana barely nodded and closed her eyes. "Lord, Duhana needs to be healed of her cancer. You're the great healer. If it's your will, we're asking for complete healing for Duhana. Amen." I released her hand before I stood back up. She did not move. I noticed that Deonte's face appeared to be disappointed.

"Thank you for the prayer. I really thought it would heal her. My family had told me of stories…" he shook his head. "I thought they were true," he said, lowering his head.

"I'm sorry. I wish the stone had worked. Put your faith in God. Not some stone," I advised. I explained I needed to get back.

"I'll walk down with you. I'm going to grab something to eat from the cafeteria," he informed me.

We walked in silence until we reached the cafeteria. I explained I was going to grab an Uber and said goodbye. He headed into the cafeteria before I moved toward the exit. The guilt of not healing her was getting to me. Perhaps Jesus was whispering in my ear. There was a sign for the restrooms. I entered and confirmed I was alone. I gazed in the mirror and concentrated on arriving invisible in Duhana's hospital room. She was alone and resting. I placed my left hand on her forehead and held her hand with my right hand. The stone warmed. It grew hotter and hotter. She opened her eyes and grabbed my right hand with her left hand. Frozen in place. I even held my breath. She removed her hand from mine and buzzed the nurse. A nurse came through the door immediately.

With her glasses at the tip of her nose, the nurse looked over them, "Duhana, it's nice to see you awake. What can I do for you?"

"Where's my brother? I need to see my brother," Duhana asked.

The nurse said she would page him. Duhana looked around the room. "I know someone, or something is here. I don't know what you did, but thank you."

My eyes filled up. I was a little choked up. Had the stone just healed her or had God? I knew God was using me and the stone to help others. Duhana sat herself up and took a sip of water. I wanted to stay and enjoy this glorious moment with her.

Deonte ran in. "Duhana, is everything okay?"

She looked up with a smile on her face and reached out for him. Deonte welcomed her embrace. Tears started streaming down both of their faces. I felt as though I was intruding on their special moment and returned home.

I plopped myself down on my bed, thinking about all the good I could do with the stone. I could heal everyone. As I daydreamed about all the amazing things I could do, I realized I could not do them. It would draw too much attention my way. Which would put the stone at risk of being taken. The fewer things I did to draw attention to myself, the better. This did not change the fact deep down I knew God had a plan for me and this stone.

All-day I was flying high as I thought about Duhana. I was unlocking my car when I heard what sounded like Juliet calling for me. I spun around and found her speed-walking toward me.

"Something must be on your mind. I've been calling you since I saw you come out of Ford Hall," she said, trying to catch her breath.

"I suppose I was in my own little world," I responded.

"Do you mind helping me with an assignment I have? I need to interview you," she explained. "Can I come over now, or do you have plans before our dinner tonight?"

Dinner? Oh, dinner. I had forgotten about the Bloom Keepers meeting. "Yes, of course," I responded.

Juliet followed me home. After a snack, we headed to my room. As I entered my room, I noticed I had missed the hamper with my outfit from my morning workout. I snatched it and tossed it into the hamper. I could feel the warmth of embarrassment on my cheeks.

Juliet sat down in one of the gold chairs and began going through her backpack. "I really appreciate this. My mother wanted me to interview her, but I figured the class didn't want to hear her talking about all the things stay-at-home mothers do."

I took off my shoes and made myself comfortable on the bed. "It surprises me you could not find someone better to interview. I'm not sure I've anything interesting to say. I'm sure she has a lot."

"Oh, you've got a lot to say. You just can't say it," she blurted. We both laughed. "So, Brooke Garrison, what's your biggest accomplishment?"

I thought about Duhana, the painting being returned, learning how to use the stone, and rescuing Kevin. None of these could be used. I began thinking about what I had accomplished before receiving the stone. I responded, "Becoming someone my mother could be proud of. After my parent's divorce, I didn't make it easy on her. My father had a drinking problem, but I didn't know it. I became more aware of it just before he died. I soon realized my mother had been trying to protect me from his toxic behavior. That's when I worked hard at making her life easier. It was the little things she appreciated, doing the dishes without being asked and cleaning up after myself. By changing my behavior, we became closer. She was less stressed, and I felt a sense of pride from making her day a little easier."

Juliet scribbled away on her pad and commented, "I don't think you told me about his drinking problem. I'm sorry you had to go through such things."

What do you say to someone when they apologize for the problems you encounter during your life? Not knowing how to respond, I waited for the next question.

"I was going to ask you about the biggest problem you encountered, but I think you answered both questions with your answer. What would you like to accomplish in the future?"

I looked at her in astonishment. "These are some pretty deep questions." This serious question needed an honest answer. "I want to make my family proud of me. My grandmother was an amazing woman who accomplished a lot in her life. I wish I could've gotten to know her better. She was an adventurous person and I really know little about that side of her. She traveled the world making friends and helping others. I would like to be more like her."

As I waited for the next question, I realized there was a lot I had not discovered about her. She and Phyllis had a lot of secrets. I wanted to know her the way Phyllis did. Losing her before she could tell me about the stone, about how to deal with this responsibility, was something I had found challenging. Juliet continued with her questioning. Thankfully, the questions became easier to answer.

Once we finished her inquisition, we had a few hours before dinner. Juliet put her things away. I stared at her for a moment. I asked, "Would you mind helping me?"

"Of course," she said as she sat up in the chair.

I asked, "I really want to find out more about my grandmother. Do you mind helping me go through the library to see if we can find anything?"

"Lead the way," she said, popping out of her seat.

We spent the next two hours going through everything in the library and learned she had an extensive book collection. We found our conversation kept reverting to Eleni Kostopoulos. Unfortunately, we didn't come up with any ideas for the meeting.

We headed downstairs and waited for the rest of the crew to arrive as we talked about Jacob and Greg. We were fortunate to have such amazing guys. I saw Greg coming up the walkway with Jacob. I let them in. Jacob appeared to have just gotten out of the shower. I asked, "Running a little late?"

His face said my statement confused him. "Your hair, it's wet." It looked as though I had embarrassed him.

Greg must have noticed it. "Don't give my boy here a hard time. He's been working out. He's going to be able to take on some bad guys in no time."

Jacob tried to hold back a smile, while Juliet leaned over and kissed him on the cheek. We chatted for a few minutes about his workouts and Juliet explained he had been working with her as well. I looked around the room at my new friends, who made up most of the Bloom Keepers. I was so proud to know them.

Phyllis called us to dinner, where we enjoyed her Chicken and Dumplings. Everyone carried in their own plate, washed it, and loaded it into the dishwasher before returning to the table to begin our meeting.

Jacob pulled out his laptop and began, "We really don't know much about Eleni Kostopoulos. She owns a lot of things in Greece and seems to have some knowledge of the stone. We don't know what she knows or who she learned it from. It looks as though she predominantly lives in this home." He flipped the screen around to allow us to see her home.

"I think Brooke and I should see what we can do to set up some surveillance and investigate her a bit. We might need you, Jacob, to do that thing you do with the computers," Greg recommended.

"I'm glad to help too if you need me," Juliet offered.

Phyllis turned to Juliet. "Enjoy the time you have to work on your studies. I'm sure with your skills, they'll need you soon enough."

Not wanting her to feel left out, "She's right. You were amazing at helping us rescue Kevin. It's thanks to you we found him. You can help with searching for her home. I think the fewer people at one time is best. Two of us at one time seems to work well."

When the meeting concluded, Phyllis provided us a Key Lime Pie for dessert. After helping her clean everything up, everyone headed home. Greg was the last to leave. I walked him to the door. He pulled me by the waist outside and shut the door behind me. "Before we get all wrapped up with Eleni, I would like to take ya on a date," he said, gazing into my eyes.

"You would huh," I said flirtatiously.

"Yes, but this is no ordinary date and I'm going to need ya help," he said, flirting back.

Curious about his statement, I responded, "Really? How can I help?"

"I'm going to need ya help to get there. I'll let you know when I have everything set up. We've got a date on Saturday. Don't make plans that day," he said before kissing me goodnight.

What could that cutie have in store for me? Feeling like I was on cloud nine, I floated to the kitchen to talk to Phyllis.

I asked Phyllis to tell me more about my grandmother. I wanted to know things only she could tell me. Phyllis made us some hot chocolates and led me to the sitting room. "I'm not sure where to start," she said, taking a sip of her drink.

"I've been afraid to ask. No one ever told me how she died. I figured it was old age, but knowing what I know now. Well, I'm certain that was not it," I responded.

Phyllis looked down at her cup and bit her lip. She looked at me and said, "I knew this day would come, and I still don't know what to tell you." She reached over and placed her hand on mine before continuing, "Your mom believes her heart failed. I don't believe that. I'm certain she was poisoned."

"Poisoned? How? She had the stone. It could heal her," I responded.

Phyllis shook her head. She reminded me, "Brooke, she didn't have the cradle to protect her."

My mind was racing. I needed answers. I asked, "If they poisoned her, why didn't this person take the stone?"

"When it happened, she and I were alone. Someone sent a bottle of wine. She believed it to be from a friend. I believe someone else sent it, but they poisoned it first. She and I were going to enjoy a steak dinner. Lillie rarely drank but wanted to celebrate because she knew you would soon receive the Bloom of Dreams. She had planned an amazing trip for you. Her plan included taking you to meet the people around the world that helped her along the way. The wine was delivered that day. She opened it and poured herself a glass. As you know, I don't drink. As soon as she took a sip, she looked at me in horror," Phyllis said, as a few tears fell from her eyes.

I ran to the bathroom to get her some tissues. She immediately wiped her eye when she received the tissue. I said, "If you're not up to telling me the rest..."

Phyllis interrupted me. "No, you need to know. Brooke, there was no doubt in my mind someone murdered her. As much as I wanted an autopsy done, I needed to discourage your mother from requesting one."

"I don't understand," I said, confused.

"If I had discovered the cause of death was murder, the police would want to know why. During an investigation, they might find out about the Bloom of Dreams. Before the ambulance arrived, I took the necklace off Lillie and put it on myself to ensure its safety. I hid it under blouses to prevent anyone from knowing I had it. It was not safe to leave it in the house," Phyllis explained. She took another sip of her hot chocolate.

"You did the right thing," I commented.

Phyllis continued, "I was not sure it was the right thing to do at that moment. I was certain the next day. I left the house to bring an outfit to the funeral home. While I was gone, someone went through the house. They tried to be discrete, but your grandmother and I are very particular about how we like things. There were a lot of things that I found out of place in our home. I held on to the necklace until the day before we went to the attorney's office. I dropped it off there to make sure he had it to give to you."

Phyllis explained she did not know who did this. She had planned to tell me, but wanted to make sure I was more familiar with the stone.

I headed to bed, thinking about my grandmother's murder. *Whoever killed her will come after me, but I will hunt for them. Unfortunately, Phyllis could not provide me with any leads. I'm sure they will eventually show themselves. For now, I needed to find out more about Eleni.*

Six

Greg advised me to be ready at 9:00 am for our date. I was to bring a light jacket for the sixty-seven-degree high. He informed me I might get dirty. I asked about footwear. Greg told me I needed something to keep my feet dry. He suggested cowboy boots. I did not own cowboy boots, but I had waterproof hiking boots. *Where's he taking me?* I could not wrap my head around what type of date this would be. I had faith he had something nice planned.

I asked Greg to come early to join us for breakfast. He arrived at 8:00 am. Phyllis made us blueberry pancakes. We had a pleasant breakfast with her. She advised me she would spend the rest of the weekend with her sister and would leave after breakfast. Greg and I did the dishes for her.

Despite trying, Greg would not tell me where we were going. We headed south toward Mount Washington. I told Greg about my grandmother's murder. He agreed they would come out of the woodwork, eventually.

We turned down a paved driveway along a fenced pasture with horses. Greg stopped and seemed to be texting someone. He continued slowly going down the long driveway to a beautiful farmhouse with a wraparound porch. *Who are we visiting?* He passed the house and headed down a dirt road toward a barn. Greg parked just outside the barn. We got out, and he grabbed a bag. We headed into the barn.

A young man wearing a cowboy hat had his back to us. He placed a saddle on a dark brown horse.

Greg said, "Hey man."

He looked over at us and said, "Hey. Good to see ya." He turned around and shook Greg's hand. "Hey there darlin', ya must be Brooke." He reached out and shook my hand.

"Brooke, this is Evan. We've been friends since middle school," Greg said as he directed his attention to the horse. "And this sweetie is Bonnie. You and she are going to become the best of friends," he informed me.

Surprised by his surprise, I said, "We're going riding? This is great!" I walked over to Bonnie and ran my hand along her face. She sniffed at me.

Evan asked me, "Have you ever ridden?"

"I rode one at the fair, but they just walked us around," I answered.

"Greg, I'm going to give her some pointers. Would ya put the other saddle on for me?" Evan asked.

Evan led the horse out of the barn. "Horses are sensitive animals. They can tell when you are nervous, so try to relax and enjoy it," he advised. He stopped Bonnie. "Before you even greet Bonnie, make sure ya relaxed. Now come and greet her," he instructed.

I walked over and said hello. Evan handed me a sugar cube to give her. She and I immediately became the best of friends. Evan explained to me the importance of mounting your horse from the left side. He had me get on and off of her to make sure I did it properly and remained calm. Evan had me stay on the horse. He handed me the reins. Evan instructed me on how to steer and stop Bonnie. "Bonnie's great with new riders. Trust her, she'll take care of ya," he complimented her.

Evan had me ride around the area. I learned to not hold on to the saddle as we walked. He complimented me on picking it up quickly. He told me how to get her to a trot. After a few minutes, he had me move to a canter. I was getting the hang of it when Greg showed up on a gray stallion wearing a cowboy hat.

Greg smiled at me and said, "Ya looking good!" He rode up next to Evan and thanked him. Evan told us to leave the horses in the pasture when we were done. He had to head to town with his grandpa. Greg said, "Okay Bonnie and Clyde, let's show this beautiful lady the beauty of Kentucky."

Bonnie and Clyde are so clever. I directed Bonnie to head in Greg's direction.

Acres of forest surrounded Evan's home. I asked, "How big is this property?"

Greg explained, "They have over 150 acres." We rode on a trail through the property. We had been riding for about an hour when we came upon a creek. Greg tied the reins to a tree and took mine from me. He helped me get off Bonnie. I tied her up. Greg grabbed a blanket and a bag from his horse. He laid the blanket on the ground and asked me to sit. He sat next to me and pulled a thermos from the bag, along with two mugs, two bottles of water, and some spoons.

Greg served me a hearty beef stew. The day was perfect. As we ate, I listened to the water trickling down the creek. Greg tapped me on my knee and pointed to a rabbit in the distance. I had not tried talking to animals. Just as I tried using telepathy to ask the rabbit to come to me. He slowly made his way closer. I questioned if it was me or the smell of the food that caught his interest. I called out to it again. The rabbit hopped a little closer. I assured the rabbit we meant no harm. It hopped all the way to the edge of our blanket. Not wanting to scare the rabbit, I explained to Greg what I was doing using telepathy. He asked me to see if it would let me pet it.

I asked the rabbit if it wanted me to pet it. It sat up and looked at me before hopping closer. I crept my hand toward it. It seemed to try to smell me. Gently, I ran my hand down the rabbit's back. He seemed to enjoy it. Greg moved his foot, and the rabbit darted off.

Greg turned to me and announced, "That was amazing!"

I agreed. We finished our meal and continued our trail ride. At this point, the fastest we had gone was a cantor. Greg told me he had faith I could handle a gallop. I trusted him. We headed into an open field and took off. Invigorating and empowering were how I would describe how it felt. As we approached the other end of the field, we slowed to a canter. I shouted to Greg, "That was fantastic!" This day was amazing. He did plan the perfect date.

We made our way back to the barn. The smell of the hay encompassed the area. Greg showed me how to remove the saddles and reins. The horses were so sweaty. Bonnie seemed to enjoy me brushing her. It amazed me when Greg called the horses, and they just followed him out to the pasture. We headed back home. I let him know how much I appreciated what he had done for me.

With a crooked smiled, he said, "Our date's not over yet."

He dropped me off and instructed me to clean up and asked me to wear warm clothes. I showered and was ready when he picked me up. He saw my light jacket and asked me to bring a winter coat, which I did. We did not drive far before we pulled into a parking lot. The name of the restaurant made me laugh. I read the sign again: Bonnie & Clyde Pizza Parlor. "There seems to be a theme today," I said.

Greg chuckled. "I thought you would find it humorous. He began, "I wanted to bring you somewhere nicer…"

I interrupted him, "I love it." I leaned over and kissed him.

Greg and I enjoyed one of the best crispy thin pizzas I have ever had. We hung out chatting about the wonderful day we had together. Greg confessed his mom made the stew. We talked about our plans for Sunday. Greg invited me to join him and his family at church, since my mother would not be back until the afternoon. I accepted the invitation.

When we got back to the truck, Greg explained he would need my help with getting us to the final event he had planned for us. We drove to a secluded area. Greg grabbed a blanket and our winter coats from the backseat. We exited the vehicle, and he helped me put my coat on. I grabbed my gloves from the pocket of the jacket. Greg did the same. Once we were both dressed, he pulled out his phone and asked me to look at a picture. It was a picture of a mountain cliff. *Where's he taking me?* I looked at him puzzled and ask, "Is this where we are going to go?"

"Yes. Trust me, you are going to love this," he said confidently.

"Okay," I said, without a clue what he had planned for us. I grabbed his arm and brought him to the location.

The terrain was rough. I slipped when we landed on the ridge, but was able to prevent myself from falling. Once I had stabilized my footing, I looked up and what I saw was the most amazing thing my eyes have ever seen. The green and purple colors in the sky were breathtaking. I was so moved by the view that it nearly brought me to tears. This was a perfect example of the beauty of God's creation.

Greg and I moved over to a rock with just enough room for both of us to sit. He brushed the snow off it. We both sat down and snuggled up together. This day was perfect. I looked at Greg and said, "Greg, I can't thank you enough for today. It was wonderful."

Greg leaned over and removed the hood of my coat from my head. He pulled the gloves off his hands and placed a hand on each side of my face, pushing my hair to the side. Greg leaned forward and placed his lips on mine. I closed my eyes and accepted it willingly. He had me in a trance. With each kiss placed on my lips, my senses heightened. His cologne was hypnotic. He moved his arms and wrapped them around me. Greg's next kiss was even more intense. I could feel his hands tighten around me. I did the same. My body tingled all over. I struggled with wanting more and knowing I wanted to wait. Never had I been in this position. Greg pulled away and put his forehead against mine. At that moment, it felt as though we were the only people in the world. He seemed to struggle, too. We were so in tune with one another. He pulled me to him and ran his arms up my back.

I wrapped my arms around him. "Greg, I love you," I assured him. I inhaled his cologne again. I leaned in and began kissing him with such passion. He kissed back, matching my intensity. Suddenly, we both pulled away from one another. Our faces resembled the expression a child would make when their parent caught them stealing a cookie from the cookie jar. We both laughed and leaned in for a hug.

"Perhaps we should head out," Greg suggested.

In a flirty way, I rolled my eyes and said, "I suppose you're right." I looked him in the eye and said, "I don't think I could be happier than I am at this moment." We began kissing again. The heat built up. Intense was how I would describe it. I pulled away and smiled. "We need to get out of here. This place is dangerous," I said, flirting again.

Seven

It was so nice worshiping with Greg and his family. We held hands. The pastor was speaking about sin. Greg's mother looked over at us several times, but I tried to keep my attention on the pastor. I was grateful for Greg, and I having self-control over one another. *I am not so sure Greg's mother thinks we have.*

After lunch, Greg and I went to my house. I called Allison. I needed to know if we could come. She asked me to give her thirty minutes. Greg and I waited thirty minutes before dropping into Allison's living room.

After a quick introduction, Allison provided me a picture of where William and Lainie were hiding out. Greg and I popped in to pay them a visit before getting Kevin. William was reading a book on the sofa when we appeared.

"You really know how to surprise someone. Where's my boy? Allison said you would bring him here," William asked.

I struggled with what to say. I took a deep breath and said, "Well, I wanted to talk to you about Kevin. Is Lainie here?"

"She ran out to the store, but she should be back soon," he informed us. He asked us to sit down.

"William, it's important you understand Kevin was tortured. We feel he should not be recovering from this trauma by himself. I know it's safer for you to remain apart, but he needs to come here. When you see him, you'll notice the sparkle of life he had in his eyes is gone. I don't feel he's capable of protecting the journal right now," I disclosed.

William's jaw dropped open and his eyes opened, showing his shock. His eyes looked frightened. He asked, "What happened to him?"

I explained what I knew. William's eyes filled. The front door flung open. A woman appeared wearing a blond wig and sunglasses. She was carrying a few bags of groceries. Greg jumped up to help the lady with her bags.

She said, "Brooke, it's nice to see you." I heard the voice. It was Lainie. Once her hands were free, she took off her glasses. We explained our concerns about Kevin. She was upset by the information as well. Lainie explained they had plenty of room for him. Everyone agreed the journal was safer being away from all of us at this point. It would remain at the villa.

We appeared in the field outside the villa. Unfortunately, when we arrived it was raining, and we sprinted to the shelter of the patio. When we walked into the villa, we looked for Isabella at the front desk. At first, I did not see her. Just as we were turning away, she sprang up from behind the counter. During a brief conversation with her, she informed us that Kevin had improved little since we last saw him. Greg filled her in on our plan to take him to a safer place. We did not want to provide details about where he was going or who he would be with. It was as much for his safety and for Leonardo and Isabella.

Greg knocked softly on my room door, which was Kevin's for the time being. The door slowly opened, revealing a man I barely recognized. Kevin looked as though he had not brushed his hair since I saw him last.

I smiled and asked, "How are you doing?" He shrugged his shoulders and did not verbally respond. "I have good news. We're taking you to your parents," I informed him.

His eyes perked up. "Really?"

We helped him pack the few things he had into a laundry bag that was hung in the closet. He told us he needed more clothes. We agreed to take him to his apartment to pick up a few things.

We arrived invisible to ensure no one would see us if anyone was there. He packed a small bag of things to take to the safe house.

When we arrived, his parents immediately showered him with hugs. He clung to them. William took his bag. Greg and I said our goodbyes and headed back to my house before my mother returned from her trip.

Sadly, Greg headed home to work on his class assignments. I did the same. After about an hour I needed a snack. I heard laughter coming from the kitchen. I stood in the doorway as I saw my mother telling Lance about her trip. The joy in her face made me smile. We hugged, and I greeted Lance. She continued her story about her weekend with Mary and Jerry. When she concluded, Lance invited me to join them for dinner. The idea no longer made me sick to think about, but I explained I had homework to complete. I grabbed a snack and headed back to the library. I was nearly done with my assignments when I heard a text come through.

JULIET: We know where you know who is going to be Saturday.

BROOKE: Meeting???

JULIET: No. Family dinner. Come see me at 11 pm.

It took me a while to get my head back to working on my final assignment. I found my mind drifting off. At first, I thought about what Juliet would tell me about Eleni. My thoughts moved to Duhana. I wanted to know about her recovery. I sat back in the chair and looked at my grandmother's book collection. This immediately changed the course of my thoughts. I needed to know who killed my grandmother.

I did not know where to start my search. All I knew was she received a bottle of wine. She was the only one to drink from it and she died immediately. I had nothing to lead me toward learning more.

At 11:06 pm, I dropped into Juliet's room. "You're late," she said from the comfort of her bed.

"Sorry, I lost track of time," I responded.

Juliet grabbed a piece of paper from her nightstand and handed it to me. "This is the address you'll need to be at Saturday night. She'll be attending a play at the National Theater in Greece. Jacob and I figured you could follow her. Then you will know where she lives, and we can try to find something to help us understand what she wants and how we can stop her. There are plenty of pictures of the theater online," she informed me. I thanked her and headed home to get some sleep.

I woke up Monday morning, anxious about Saturday. I knew it was going to be a long week. My exercise routine was more vigorous than normal. Pushing myself helped keep my mind off Eleni and what she had done to Kevin. I even met up with several classmates to stay focused on my studies.

Thursday, I wanted revenge for what Eleni had done to Kevin. I knew this was not healthy. After praying about it, God put it on my heart to check on Duhana. Perhaps I needed some good news. I headed over when I knew Deonte should be home.

Not knowing where she lived, I went to Deonte's house. I hoped he would be home and could fill me in on how she was doing. Fortunately, she had been staying with him. Deonte invited me in. I found Duhana sitting on the sofa, playing with Ozzy. She explained to me they had thought they needed the stone to heal her. She said, "Nothing happened when you touched me." *What? That's not possible.* "We were certain it would heal me, but it didn't." Duhana put Ozzy on the ground and leaned toward me. "The most amazing thing happened when you left. God sent an angel to answer our prayers. I was healed. Each day I am getting stronger and stronger," she informed me.

Deep down I felt like she was correct. Jesus healed her. When the angel visited, I understood the stone was a gift from God. I was going to let God use me. I knew I would not be perfect, but I would do the best I could to do His will. We talked for quite a while about the power of God and how he had moved in our lives.

I left there feeling much better. The rest of the evening was spent focusing on finishing my last assignment. I headed to bed early.

Friday morning, Juliet and I headed to the park to work on Kapu Kuʻialua. She brought two bamboo sticks with her. Juliet began by showing me pressure points and how to take down someone. When we started, we had a few people watch us and they quickly moved on. Once we started battling with the bamboo, we built up quite the crowd. She had taught me well. Juliet came after me. Our sticks collided. We struck one another many times. As we moved toward the crowd, they moved back out of our way.

Juliet jumped in the air and fell on me. I lost my footing. She took that opportunity to sweep her stick behind my legs. My body crashed to the ground. Before I knew it, she was on top of me with her stick at my throat.

The audience cheered her on. She took her foot off me and extended her hand to me to help me up. We both had a good laugh. We grabbed our water bottles and spoke with a few people in the crowd. A couple carrying a volleyball tapped Juliet on the shoulder.

She immediately turned around and smiled. After they greeted one another, she introduced them to me. Michael and Missy knew her from the University. They described Juliet as being quiet and never expected her to be someone with such skills. They were right. I didn't know what she was capable of until I met her in Greece. On the drive back, she informed me Jacob had learned a lot since she first started working with him. She felt Greg's training was helping him as well.

That evening, Lance joined us for dinner. I learned more about him during our game of Hand and Foot. Mom and I had not played this card game since moving to Kentucky. I have always enjoyed spending an evening playing. It was a great distraction. We did not finish playing until after 11:00 pm.

I woke refreshed and spent the day shopping with my mother. She had bought me a few new outfits and found some lovely clothes for herself. After lunch, I headed to my room and took a quick nap to make sure I was well-rested before following Eleni.

I arrived at the theater invisible. It took me a while to find her. She had a balcony seat. I teleported over to her. Eleni was with an attractive man. Both seemed to enjoy the show. It was not long before the show was over. She stood up and told the man they were leaving. She walked out and two men were waiting just outside the balcony door. As soon as the couple strolled past them, they began following them. When they made it to the exit door, one man went outside. He walked up to a car and opened the car door for them. The other man escorted them to the vehicle. Once they were in the vehicle, the two men jumped in the car behind hers. One in the front seat and the other in the back. I placed myself in the back seat next to the man. We rode through the streets of Athens for a short while. There was a lot of traffic. We arrived at a port. Everyone got out and boarded a yacht.

I moved to the stern and followed the couple inside. There was a couch with a powder blue fabric. A wood tabletop with a star inlaid in the center. It rested in front of the couch. There was wood on the ceiling. The two men stayed outside. Eleni and the man with her on the balcony entered the cabin.

The deck was matched by the ceiling. To the right was a bar and to the left was a sitting area. A crème-colored sofa had blue and pink throw pillows. There was a trunk and a chair with pink squiggly lines. The walls were lined with high gloss wood. Just past the sitting area

53

was a table for four. The wood was just as shiny as that on the walls. It was not my style, but tastefully decorated.

The man grabbed a drink from the bar. Eleni looked over at him. "I'm tired. Leave when you're done with your drink," Eleni muttered.

I followed her down a narrow wooden stairwell. There were several wooden doors on that landing. Her room was to the left of the stairs. This room was larger than I expected to see on a vessel. The floor was white marble. Her room was a beautiful cabin. A bed was in the center of the room. It had a white fabric headboard that was mounted to the structure. Along the wall was a cabinet that stretched along the wall with many drawers. Above them were three oval windows.

She grabbed some pajamas and walked to the head. I heard the shower turn on. *Time to get nosey. Where to start?* I opened her closet and found some extremely expensive clothes. There was nothing of significance there. I went through the drawers and still found nothing. Eleni's purse caught my eye. She had placed it on the dresser. I started going through it. I found her identification. It had a Corfu address. The sound of water suddenly stopped. She was getting out of the shower. I put everything back in her purse and headed home.

With her out of her home, we had at the very least, the night to search her house. I called Jacob and told him I had an emergency. Juliet and he were on a date. They told me they would meet me in Jacob's room. I texted Greg to see if he could go with me. He could not join us. He was with his family at his grandmother's home.

I waited to go to Jacob's room until I heard from them. When the message eventually came, I rushed over immediately. I explained the situation to them and provided Jacob the address of her home. He found a photo of the house. The property was amazing. She had waterfront property on the island of Corfu. The three of us headed over together to cover more ground. The home had a pool and a beautiful Greek garden. We arrived in the garden and did not see anyone. The house had many large windows, which made it easy to see inside the home. We transported inside. Each of us took separate areas of the home.

I went straight to her bedroom. The décor in the room surprised me. Pale gray was the primary color of the room. The room had a wonderful view of the ocean. The room was stunning but not as large as a mansion in the states. There was a small desk in the corner. On the desk were a few books and a laptop. I needed Jacob. I looked in a mirror on the wall and began picturing the various rooms of the home I had seen on my way to her bedroom to see if I could locate him. He was in the home theater. The room had a large screen on the far wall and three layers of couches. Each on a different level. I popped in and grabbed him without saying a word. I took him back to the bedroom.

"Jacob, I need you to work on the computer. We'll continue searching," I instructed. He immediately turned the computer on to get to work.

My search continued through the house. I turned up nothing. I was heading to another bedroom when I saw Juliet sitting at a desk in her office. The room was a large room with light-colored tile and a pale blue rug. White bookshelves covered the walls above the cabinets. A white desk was in the center of the room. Two dark blue chairs sat on the other side of the desk.

Her focus was on an ancient book. I cleared my throat and asked, "Did you find something?"

"Yes. Come look at this," she instructed. Juliet turned the book around. It looked ancient. "I don't know what it says, look it's written in Greek, but…" She flipped the pages and pointed at a drawing. It was a drawing of the Bloom of Dreams in its cradle.

I began reading aloud to Juliet. The book talked about a mysterious jewel that a magical wood nymph named Echo had enchanted. She lived in the mountains, rivers, streams, lakes, and forests. The god Pan fell madly in love with Echo, but she did not want to have anything to do with him. Pan was so angry he used his powers to panic the shepherds. They went mad and killed Echo. They believed her soul was placed in the stone, which is why it had magical powers. Those with Echo's soul held great power.

Juliet, "We now understand why she wants it. Do you think this story is true?"

"I've never been one to believe in Greek gods. I believe Jesus gave it the power it holds." As I closed the book, I said, "Eleni's Greek, I'm sure she believes in this Greek god's story." I quickly told her about the angel that came to me. I looked around the room, "Let's see if we can find anything about her plan to get it"

We continued searching her home. Juliet could not read any of the papers. She moved on to other rooms and I took over the search of the office. I discovered information about Kevin and his family.

Eleni had been receiving reports about them from Spiro Hallas, which included information about their travels, addresses, and connections. Juliet and I met up with Jacob. He explained he had been having a difficult time because everything was in Greek. I took the necklace off and placed it around Jacob's neck.

"Wow! This is amazing," he said as he began typing away. Juliet and I waited for Jacob to finish his work. Once finished, he returned the necklace to me, and we returned to his room.

"Thank you for your help. We've learned a lot," I said.

"That was so cool how the necklace changed the language on the screen," Jacob said, gleamingly. "Is this how you feel all the time?"

I smiled, knowing exactly how he was feeling. "We need to figure out how to stop her from coming after it again. She seemed to believe in Greek mythology. Maybe we should start our research there."

"That's a good idea. Let's meet Monday after class at the library," Juliet suggested.

"Great idea. Jacob, would you research Spiro Hallas? He's the one providing Eleni with information about Kevin and his family. I suspect about me too," I said.

I headed home and finished my homework before heading to bed.

Eight

Monday afternoon, we met in the library at 3:30 pm to review any new information we had on Eleni's plans. Juliet, Greg, and I showed up on time. Juliet had tried to contact Jacob several times but had not heard back from him. She explained, "Jacob told me he was working on something and would be here as soon as he can. He did find Spiro Hallas. He has a picture of him as well." Juliet looked at the window next to the door to the room we were in.

"I don't have anything to report," I added.

Greg chimed in, "I've been a little busy this weekend with my dad. I got nothing."

My phone buzzed.

UNKNOWN: Jam at 5:00 pm Galt House Hotel

I told everyone about it and asked if they wanted to go. Greg said he had to head home and could not make it. Juliet said she was interested, but did not think she was ready for it yet.

The door to the room flew open. Jacob came in with his computer in his hand. He kicked the door shut behind him. He dropped his bag on the floor and opened his computer. "Sorry, I'm late, but I think you will understand in a moment," he said while tapping away on his keyboard. He turned the computer around and showed us a picture of a man. "This is Spiro Hallas. He's Eleni's historian, or she refers to him that way. Spiro has extensive knowledge of Greek mythology, and he's excellent at researching things."

Jacob started walking around the room as he provided the information to us. "Before our meeting, I checked her computer,

57

hoping to find some more information for us," he said dramatically, he grabbed the back of an empty chair and leaned forward. "You know what I found. She was on a video call with our new person of interest. Yes, Spiro. He informed Eleni he had just arrived in the states. Any guesses where he landed?"

Greg seemed annoyed by Jacob's presentation, Greg commented sarcastically, "Louisville."

Jacob pointed his finger at Greg and said, "You'd be correct. He told Eleni he had your schedule and will check in when he has either the necklace or something else to report."

"Brooke, I think we should try to make sure you have one of us with you as you change classes. Maybe you should come in with Greg," Juliet suggested.

"I really don't think that's necessary. There are too many people here for them to do anything. I need to be more alert when I am in the parking lot or if I am in a secluded area," I replied.

"Brooke's right. She has the skills and knowledge, not to mention she'll have the stone with her," Greg agreed.

We ended our meeting, and Greg walked me to my car. I told him I was going to the jam downtown and would head straight home afterward. We kissed each other and headed our separate ways. I drove to a drive-through and got a bottle of water and a small order of nuggets to tide me over till dinner.

I left everything in the vehicle except my car key. Only a few people were standing in a group outside the Galt House Hotel. I walked up to them and asked, "Are you guys here for the jam?"

A blond man nodded at me. He looked me up and down and said, "I'm Josh. This isn't for beginners. Are you sure you're up for this?"

"I guess we'll see," I replied. *Well, I'm hoping not to kill myself.*

One of the other men with him said, "Don't mind him. I'm David. Josh just hates to see people get hurt."

We waited around till 5:15 pm and, like clockwork; they started running. *I guess I just go.* We made our way to the hotel garage. One by one, each of them climbed up the wall. *Don't think. Just go.* I scaled the building. Once I reached the roof. I looked and saw them heading down the other side. I sprinted across it to catch up with them. We descended. David looked back at me. It was more difficult going down than up. Once I reached the bottom, David hollered, "This way!"

I looked in his direction. Everyone was crossing the road. Josh was leading the group. I caught up with David and another man. They both froze when a car slammed on the brakes. I slid across the hood of the vehicle and was no longer in the rear. I actually passed another man as we headed up the VA's Regional Office building. We continued moving from one building to another. Gliding through every obstacle in our path. Whether it be on a building, along the sidewalk area, or on a car. The path Josh lead us down eventually brought us back to the hotel. When I caught up with Josh and the other man in front of me, I could hear sirens in the distance. David arrived just after me.

"Impressive, Brooke. You're welcome to join us anytime. It's time to go. I hear the Po-Po. I'm sure they're looking for us," Josh said, heading into the garage.

David and the other man also provided compliments. I said a quick goodbye to them and headed to my car. I needed to get out of the area quickly. I had not noticed my hands being all scratched up from the bricks until I grabbed my steering wheel. At the first light, I came to, I chugged some water and glanced at my phone. It showed a missed call from Greg. I called and spoke with him about the experience I had with this group. When I arrived home, I showered before heading to dinner. Phyllis and mom were already at the table when I arrived.

Once I sat, Mom said grace. I grabbed my napkin and placed it on my lap before asking them how their day was. Mom replied, "It was hectic, but I was able to finish most of my big projects before I left today. I may need to work some evenings this week. We are gaining another company next week, so don't expect me home for dinner the rest of the week."

I asked, "Well, that's no fun. Do you want me to drop dinner off for you?"

"It's unnecessary. They bring food in for us when this happens," she said, taking another bite of lasagna.

"I had lunch with a friend from church," Phyllis added.

We continued catching up. It was probably best not to mention my jam downtown. After dinner, we all helped with the dishes. I excused myself to work on my homework assignments. I wanted to get ahead of my assignments in case I had some unforeseen interruptions. My phone chimed.

GREG:	U busy?
BROOKE:	Not really. What's up?
GREG:	Want to go for a stroll?
BROOKE:	I'll meet you out front.

I grabbed my jacket and slipped on my boots. I texted my mother to let her know I was going out with Greg. When I opened the front door, Greg was standing there with a hot chocolate. I gave him a hug and a kiss. We started walking down the street. Greg apologized to me for being so absent lately. He explained his father wanted to do something nice for his mother.

I stopped and turned to him; he looked as though he was about to cry. I asked, "What's wrong?"

Greg seemed to struggle with telling me.

"You don't have to tell me," I informed him.

"I need to tell you. My mom... My mom has endometrial cancer," he said, choking back tears.

I took our cups and placed them on the ground. I turned to him. He reached out to me and pulled me into him and began weeping. When he could compose himself, he released me and wiped his eyes. I grabbed our cups, and we started heading back toward our houses.

He asked, "Dad and I have been working over at my grandpa's house on a project for Mom. I need a favor from you. Would you do something with my mom and Karen on Saturday to get her out of the house for a few hours?"

"Sure. I would love to get to know her and Karen better," I assured him.

"I don't want to say much about what we have planned for her. I want you to see it when she does. Karen knows what's going on. Dad's going to give you some money to cover whatever you decide to do with her," he informed me. We said our goodbyes. I went up and continued working until I was too tired to continue.

I kept an eye out for Spiro when I left for class the next day. I found myself distracted in class. Bob, another student, who I would describe as our class clown, could not keep his eyes off Sharon. She was a beautiful, shy girl. I had watched him try to do everything he could to get her to notice him in class. Yet, he seemed too shy to ask her out. When he was not paying attention, Sharon would sneak a glimpse of him. They both seemed interested in one another.

I decided to see what I could do to help them. Sharon needed to let Bob know she was interested. I caught him staring at her. Using my powers of persuasion, I told Karen to look at Bob and smile, which she did. Bob provided an awkward smile back. He seemed surprised by her action.

"Ms. Garrison. Excuse me," our professor tried to get my attention. The student behind me tapped me on the back with what I presume was a pen. Confused, I looked up.

"Ms. Garrison, please tell us which of these is the correct answer. Read the question with the correct answer," she said, pointing to the question.

I looked at the board and studied the answers. I said, "The trial, in which Ms. Jones was accused of conspiracy was scheduled to end that very week."

"Very good. That is the correct answer because it is one particular thing," she explained.

My attention was back on Bob and Sharon. Just as class was about to be dismissed, I tried to persuade Bob to stop her before she left the class. When the professor dismissed us. I did not run out like I normally would. I wanted to keep encouraging Bob. In a bashful way, he walked up to Sharon. She seemed to have a hard time making eye contact with him. I heard Bob introduce himself. I told him to ask her out. He did. Sharon seemed terrified to answer. Come on Sharon. *You can say yes.* I boosted her ego by telling her she was beautiful. I also told her this may be her only chance to go out with him. Sharon replied in a bashful way, "Sure."

Bob asked with some confidence, "Are you available now?"

"Yes," she replied, blushing.

My phone vibrated.

JACOB: I'm outside your building. We need to talk. Where are you?

I grabbed my things and headed out of the class. At a fast pace, I made my way to the front of the building. Jacob was looking around the area. His gaze met me as I walked up to him.

I asked, "What's up?"

Jacob pulled me away from the main pathway. "Eleni is arriving Saturday. You need to be at the airport to follow her. She's meeting up with Spiro," he whispered.

"Sure. What time?" I replied.

"She'll be here at 1:00 pm. This is where you need to be," he said, handing me a piece of paper.

I reached for it and quickly pulled my hand back. "I can't make it. Greg has something big planned for his mother. He has asked me to help get her out of the house. I'll be with her and Karen all day," I explained.

"Can't you get out of it? Greg would understand," Jacob pleaded.

I took a deep breath and thought about how important this seemed to him. I also considered what she was going through right now. "No, I can't." We both seemed to assess the situation. "I've got an idea. I don't want to say anything yet. When I have something figured out. I will let you know."

We went our separate ways. Since this was my last class for the day, I headed home.

It was just Phyllis and me for dinner. I ran my idea by her to see what she thought. "If I give Juliet the Bloom of Dreams and the compact mirror, she can follow Eleni. That way, I can keep my commitment to Greg, and we can still find out what Eleni's up to."

"Juliet has proven to be trustworthy. You said she's also able to protect herself. I don't think it's a bad idea," Phyllis agreed.

After dinner, I called Juliet to see if I could stop by. She explained she was out and would stop by shortly. I was working on my homework when I heard Juliet knock on the door frame to my room.

"I didn't hear the bell. Come on in," I instructed.

Juliet made her way to the chair and sat down. "Is everything okay?"

I asked, "Did Jacob tell you about Eleni flying in on Saturday?"

"Yes. He said he was going to tell you about it after class," she answered.

I questioned, "Have you spoken with him since I met with him?"

Juliet shook her head, "No. Why?"

Without going into much detail, I explained the pickle I was in, followed by my plan. Confused, Juliet looked at me. "Let me get this straight. Do you want me to wear the Bloom of Dreams and follow Eleni by myself? Have you lost your mind?"

"Actually, I think it's was a brilliant plan, and Phyllis agrees with me. Juliet, you have proven you're a master of Kapu Ku'ialua. You know what the stone can do and how it works. All you need to do is be at the airport when she arrives. You'll need to be invisible. Look into her vehicle and teleport there when it's safe. You need to eavesdrop on her and Spiro. Find out as much as you can and report back to the Bloom Keepers your findings," I encouraged.

"Maybe Jacob can come with me," Juliet muttered.

"That would be too dangerous. It would be easier to be detected. Besides, if you need to get in the car with her to listen in on their conversation, there might not be enough room for you both. No, you should go by yourself. He's not ready for something like this yet either," I discouraged.

"I suppose you're right," she said.

I took the necklace off and handed it to her. "Put it on. We are going to see how well you spy on Phyllis. I'll stand back and watch. She's probably still in the sitting room. I want you to sit next to her on the couch without being detected. Bring me to the foyer," I instructed as I grabbed Juliet's arm.

Phyllis was reading her book. Juliet tiptoed into the sitting room and gently set down next to her on the sofa. She stayed squished up at the other end. I quietly made my way to the kitchen pantry and called Phyllis, "Juliet and I are hungry. Do you have anything for us to snack on?"

Phyllis replied, "There's some apple pie left from the other night. Would you like me to bring you a few slices?"

"We'll come down for it. I would like you to join us. Let me know when it's ready. Thanks," I said before hanging up. I moved to an area of the kitchen to make sure I would not be in her way.

Phyllis walked past me and opened the refrigerator. She placed the pie in the oven to warm it.

Juliet moved in front of the refrigerator after Phyllis poured three glasses of water. She took them to the dining room, along with some silverware. Juliet remained in her spot, pinned up against the refrigerator. Phyllis nearly detected Juliet when she went to grab the vanilla ice cream. Juliet reacted and slid out of her way just in time. Phyllis made each of us a plate with a slice and topped it with the ice cream. She took them to the dining room before calling me. My phone rang.

Phyllis looked in my direction and said, "Brooke?"

I explained to Juliet how to make us visible again. She did as I instructed. I apologized to Phyllis for not letting her in on our training session. We discussed how the training went.

"You did very well, Juliet. I didn't know you were even near me," Phyllis complimented.

Juliet handed the necklace back to me and told me she would get it from me on Saturday before I had to leave. We discussed a few more things about the stone before she went home. It was still early. I thought I would call Mechelle and see how she was doing.

"I made a friend, but she's not you. She's sweet but a little odd. She brought home chicken nuggets and did not eat them all. When I left her dorm, she had them sitting on the table. I went back two days later, and they were still there. I was going to throw them out, and she made me stop and came over and ate one," Mechelle explained.

We discussed summer break. The idea of a group vacation sounded like fun. We agreed to look into ideas and discuss them in a week or so. I really enjoyed my conversation with her. I looked on the internet for a while to see if I could find a good idea for a trip. It was difficult knowing what activities or places to go when we had not decided who would join us.

Greg and I had not talked all day. I knew he had plans to work on the surprise he and his father had for his mother after class. He promised to make time for me after Saturday. I called him. "I know you are probably exhausted, but I wanted to say good night," I said.

Sounding out of breath, Greg said, "That's sweet. I'm sorry, I meant to call when I had dinner, but dad showed up with a pizza, and we ate while we kept working. We're still here. Dad and I are almost done. We should be finished by tomorrow night."

"You're still there. I'm going to say good night then. I don't want you to stay later because of me. Have a good night. I love you," I said.

"Love ya, too," Greg said before hanging up. I knew it was best not to let him know about Juliet's mission. He had enough on his mind.

Nine

I spent all week looking for Spiro and had not seen him at all. After showering, I got ready for the day I had planned for Joann and Karen. Juliet stopped by and picked up the necklace. It felt so strange not wearing it. They were told I would pick them up at 10:00 am. When I was on my way to get them, I sent Greg a text.

I had not seen Joann in a while. She seemed less perky than normal. The only instructions I gave them were to be hungry when I arrived. Our first stop was brunch. I took them to a restaurant called Toast on Market. I read the reviews which were good. The menu had a large variety of things to choose from. I ordered lemon soufflé pancakes, which had their signature lemon ricotta pancake topped with blueberry compote and creamy vanilla custard, which was amazing.

Joann and I got to know one another better at brunch. She was honest and told me about her cancer. Her surgeries were scheduled for next week. I wondered why Greg never asked me to heal her. He knows I could do it. I paid the check and took them to our second destination for the day.

We arrived at the Serenity Spa. Joann turned to me and said, "Seriously? This I'm going to enjoy."

"Joann, you are getting the Farmhouse Fresh Relaxation Treatment, and Karen and I will get the Farmhouse Fresh Body Scrub. We had a choice of a sugar or salt scrub. I chose sugar," I said.

Karen and I were in the same room. We did not talk. Both of us lay there relaxing. I had not had this much peace in a long time. I even dozed off for a few minutes. We finished before Joann did, which gave Karen and me the opportunity to talk for a few minutes. She was very excited about the surprise they had for Joann. She was tight-lipped about the surprise. Joann came out looking like a new person. She and an employee of the spa were laughing as they exited the room.

"I feel like a new person," Joann boasted.

"You look amazing," I said as I felt my phone buzz.

JULIET: I'm heading over. Wish me luck.

BROOKE: Good luck. Just a reminder, leave your phone at home.

It was nearly 1:00 pm. Not knowing what time to return, I texted Greg to see if he knew when I should return.

GREG: 45 minutes

We piled in the car. "One more stop on the ladies about the town tour," I informed them.

"I've really enjoyed today. It has been wonderful getting to know you better," Joann commented.

"I agree. We should do this again when my mother and Phyllis can join us," I replied. I pulled into a frozen yogurt store and took them in for a treat. I did not know what Andrew had planned for them, but I was certain they would want an early dinner.

As I ate, I could not help but think about Juliet. I wondered if she had found any information out and if she was able to remain undetected. It was frustrating not having the stone to pop in and check on the status. I took another bite of my frozen yogurt and the pain in my head became unbearable.

"Brooke, are you okay?" Karen inquired.

I lowered my head in pain and closed my eyes for a moment. I looked up and replied, "Brain freeze." Everyone had a good laugh.

GREG: We are ready. You can park on the curb in front of the house.

I did as Greg instructed. We started walking up the path. Karen was walking next to her mother. I tapped her on the shoulder and motioned for her to let her mother go first. We were let in by Joann.

I was expecting a bunch of people jumping out yelling surprise. Greg and Andrew had not greeted us.

Karen said, "Mom, close your eyes." Karen grabbed her hand and led her to the back door. "Watch your step." Karen assisted her mother on to the deck. Greg and Andrew were in the yard. Andrew held up three fingers. Every second, he dropped one of them. After the last finger, Greg, Karen, and Andrew yelled, "Surprise!"

They moved out of her way to allow her to see their gift in the backyard. Joann's mouth dropped open, and her eyes filled with tears. Andrew started to tear up, too. It looked like Greg and Karen were fighting back the tears as well. I know I was.

Joann turned to me and said, "I have a she-shed." She swiftly made her way to it. It was a wooden shed, and the inside was adorable. It had a cream-colored sofa with some accent pillows and a few chairs. Windowpanes for decorations. It was a shabby chic style. In the back was a bookcase with a few books.

"I need to show you a unique feature," Andrew announced. There was a long window along one wall. It unlatched at the top and folded down to make a counter.

Joann hugged Andrew, sobbing. I leaned over to Karen. I said, "I think she loves it." Karen smiled back. Joann made her rounds, making sure she hugged and thanked everyone.

Joann sat down to enjoy the shed that was designed with her in mind. We all eventually did the same. Greg sat next to me on the sofa. He whispered, "Dad's sorry he forgot to give you money. He said he'll give it to me tomorrow unless you must have it tonight." I let him know it was not a problem.

As predicted, Andrew announced he was hungry and would order Chinese. When the food arrived, I discovered he had ordered several items for a large variety. Joann said she would not let us eat in her shed out of fear it would get dirty. She seemed pleased with her gift.

Greg and I sat on the patio. We had a moment alone. He asked, "Ya seem distracted. Is there anything I can help with?"

"I'm concerned about Juliet. With all you had going on this week, I thought it best not to bother you. Juliet's on a mission," I said when Greg interrupted me.

"A mission... where?"

"Eleni arrived today. She's meeting up with Spiro. We need to find out what's going on. I gave you my word to be here today. Juliet's spying on Spiro and Eleni," I confessed.

Greg smiled, "I trust your judgement. Is she just following them and listening to their conversations?"

I confirmed he was correct and explained she had not returned yet. It was killing me not knowing what was going on.

Greg asked, "Is she going back to your house when she's done?"

"Yes," I said. I took a sip of my drink.

Greg stood up and held out his hand. "Let's go," he instructed.

Confused, I took his hand and followed him. Before leaving his house, Greg told his mother he would be back shortly to help clean up. She told him she would take care of it. We walked back to my house. "I'm going to wait with ya," he informed me.

I left Greg in the library. Juliet was going to return to my room. My mother would not approve of Greg being in my room with the door shut. I wrote a note on the mirror with some lipstick explaining I was in the library.

I returned to Greg. We caught up on everything that had been going on during the week. "Sweetie, thank you for the opportunity to spend such a special day with your mother. We had a wonderful day." I tried not to bring it up, but my lack of understanding about why he did not ask for help about his mother boggled my mind. I inquired, "Why haven't you asked me to heal your mother?"

Greg looked down as though he was looking for something. He took a deep breath. He looked up and said, "I promised my mom I wouldn't tell anyone about her illness. She wanted to tell people in her own time. Besides, how could you do it without her knowing?"

"Let me worry about it..." I was interrupted with Juliet walking in. "Juliet!" I jumped up and hugged her. When I released my hold on her, I noticed Jacob standing in the doorway. I pulled him into the room and shut the library door.

"I'll tell you everything, but can I get something to eat and drink?"

"Yes, of course," I bolted downstairs to see what I could scrounge up for her. My mother was sitting at the dining room table. She appeared to be working.

I stopped and asked, "How did things go today?"

Mom looked up. She muttered, "Um, busy. Can we talk later?"

I nodded. "I'm going to grab a snack," I spurted as I darted into the kitchen. An examination of the pantry revealed a granola bar and some chips. I grabbed the granola bar, a water, and some grapes for her.

As I exited the kitchen, my mother stopped me again. She looked at my neck and said, "Where's your necklace?

"I took it off to clean it. I must've forgotten to put it back on," I said, without waiting to see if she had more questions.

I had never seen Juliet scarf food as she did at that moment. *Hurry up. I need to know what happened.* I do not believe I have ever felt so impatient.

Jacob's eyes were big as he watched her devour the food.

She chugged some water and said, "I want to start by saying. This stone's so cool. They never knew I was there. I found Eleni at the airport. I glanced inside the limo that picked her up and did as you said. We drove to a house. Spiro must have rented it or something. Spiro has been spying on you all along. He knows your schedule. He even saw you downtown with a few guys running up and down buildings." She took another swig of her water.

Greg asked, "Did you find out their plan?"

"Spiro, put a tracker on your car. We saw you come out of the yogurt shop. They were going to get you then, but they noticed you were not wearing the necklace. They came here, but your mother and Phyllis were home. She dropped Spiro off at the house and she went to a hotel. They plan on getting it when you are leaving church tomorrow," she concluded.

Greg turned to me and said, "What time do I need to be here to go with you tomorrow?"

I smiled. His need to protect me was comforting. Juliet gave me the necklace and asked me to bring them back to Jacob's room, which I did.

Ten

Greg showed up a few minutes early for church. We waited in the sitting room for my mother. She was running a few minutes late. "I looked for the tracker Spiro put on ya car, but I didn't see it. After church, I'll get a better look," Greg informed me.

"Thanks, but I think we should leave it," I advised. Greg's face showed he was confused by my comment. "Hear me out. They're going to try and get it no matter where I am. It's better to be anticipating it. Also, I would rather this happen sooner than later," I explained.

Mom entered the room and asked, "Are we ready to go?"

As we piled into my mother's car, I noticed Greg, like myself, was looking around for Spiro and Eleni. We both continued surveying the road for them. Using telepathy, Greg and I communicated. Neither of us saw them. We found our seats in the church. The morning had been uneventful. Pastor Ellis's sermon was on Colossians 4:2-6. He explained we needed to devote ourselves to prayer. I knew I needed to work on this.

Greg bumped me with his elbow. Using telepathy I asked, "What?"

"Eleni just walked in. She's sitting in the back row," he informed me.

The stone did not warn me about her. She must not be going to do anything at this moment. I thought it was not smart to look in her direction. Surely, she was watching me. When the church was dismissed, Mom was talking to the lady in charge of the coffee bar. I looked around for Eleni but did not see her. Greg and I waited patiently for Mom to finish. The pastor's wife, Barbara, stopped to welcome Greg to the church. Mom greeted her when she finished her conversation. Most of the congregation had left when we made our way out of the church.

Mom suggested we go out for lunch. We went to a small diner. As I exited the vehicle, the stone had begun to heat up. I pointed to the stone to let Greg know. He looked around and shrugged. I did not see either of them.

We sat down and placed our order. There were a few other customers in the restaurant. The stone was still warm. A man sat at our only empty chair. "Hello, little lady," he said in a Greek accent. I knew it was Spiro.

The server arrived and addressed Spiro first, "Good morning, I'm Rosie, can I get you something to drink?"

Greg turned to our server and said, "No. He's not staying." Spiro glared at Greg.

"Careful, this does not concern you," Spiro advised.

My mother looked puzzled, "Can we help you?"

Spiro dismissed her question, "You little lady are going to come with me if you don't want to see your beautiful mother harmed.

Greg leaned over toward him, "She's not going anywhere with ya."

"Boy, if you know what's good for you, you'll back off," Spiro said leaning toward Greg.

"Perhaps I'm not as wise as ya would hope," Greg said firmly as he leaned closer.

I looked over at Mom. She looked terrified. Using persuasion, I talked him into leaving. My mother was silent after we ordered our food. She seemed to be playing on her phone, which was odd.

Without warning, she blurted, "What do you think he wanted?"

We were interrupted when Rosie brought us our food. "I have no idea. He's gone now. Let's just enjoy our breakfast," I suggested.

"How can you be so dismissive? I think he wanted to kidnap you right here in broad daylight," Mom said, frazzled.

"I'm sure he's gone. Don't worry, Ms. Davis, I'll stay with her until we are sure he's gone. Besides, even if I'm not around, he has no idea how dangerous Brooke can be. She can easily take care of herself now," Greg commented.

For the rest of lunch, we all remained rather quiet. The stone was not as hot. Spiro must have been outside. Mom paid for lunch. Using telepathy, I told Greg he was still around. We walked out of the restaurant, holding hands. I inspected the parking lot but did not discover Spiro or Eleni.

When we reached the house, Greg turned to my mother and said, "I think that guy from the diner is gone. I'm going to stay with Brooke just to be safe." He turned to me, "The guys are going hatchet throwing. I thought you would enjoy that."

"Just keep an eye on her. Oh, and keep an eye out for that evil man," Mom commented.

I ran up to change out of my church clothes, and Greg decided to do the same. The stone was still warm. I called Juliet and filled her in before heading downstairs. She said she was going to let Jacob know. She planned to meet us.

Greg picked me up. I told him Juliet, and possibly Jacob would be joining us as well. During our trip, the stone never cooled down. The place was busy. We had to park at the back of the building. I had opened my door when a car pulled up behind his truck, blocking the truck in. The stone became very hot.

Spiro stepped out of the vehicle. "Brooke, your mother's safety is at risk. I suggest you come with me," he instructed.

Greg lunged forward and shouted, "She's not going anywhere with ya!"

Spiro pulled out his phone and showed me a video of my mother. She was in her room on the phone. She was still wearing her church clothes. She did not seem aware anyone was with her.

He pulled the phone away, "Get in the car!"

I looked over at Greg and said, "I'm sorry. I must go. Someone's with my mother." I jumped in his car. Greg hopped in his car as we drove off.

Spiro told me to put some handcuffs on and he put a hood over my face. I did as he instructed. Using telepathy, I told Greg to go help my mother. He never replied. I did not know if he had received my message. The hood let zero light in. We drove for a few minutes. The vehicle stopped. I heard Spiro get out. The door next to me opened. He pushed me over and grabbed my phone from my pocket. It sounded like he dropped it on the ground and stomped on it. I sensed him approaching me. I knew he wanted the necklace. I pulled myself away from his grasp. Flipping my feet to be able to kick him. I pushed as hard as I could with my legs. He must have hit the car door and fallen to the ground. It sounded as though he was just outside the car door. The door slammed shut. I heard someone get back into the front seat. The car started moving again.

I thought about pulling my hands out of the handcuffs, but I felt it best not to use the powers of the stone yet. There was no telling what they knew it could do. We drove for about ten minutes before someone pulled me out of the backseat and took the hood off of me. The light blinded me for a moment. It was Spiro. I was standing in a garage. He told me to walk and shoved me towards a door. I walked into the home. I was forced into a basement. One without windows. He followed me down the stairs. I noticed a shackle on the floor. Spiro placed the hoody back on me. It sounded as though he grabbed the chain that was mounted to the floor, I felt him shackle my foot. I heard his footsteps as he made his way up the stairs. The sound of a door locking could be heard.

I concentrated on pulling my hands through the handcuffs. I pulled the hood off myself and pulled my foot out of the shackle. *Spiro, it's time I find out what you are up to.* I pulled my mirror from my bra. I had a feeling I would need to keep it secure. I was grateful he did not search me better. I opened the mirror and pictured myself just outside the garage invisible. I heard Spiro on the phone. I walked toward his voice. He was in the kitchen.

"I was surprised she didn't fight me more. She's in the basement," he told the person on the other end of the call. There was a pause. "Yes, I have her locked up. When will you be here?" he said rolling his eyes. Another pause. "Two hours. Seriously? Bring something for me to eat. I'm starving," Spiro said before hanging up the phone. He went into the living room and turned the television on before making himself comfortable on the sofa.

I looked around the house to see if I could find anything of importance. I discovered nothing. I walked through the front door. The number on the house was 1534. I walked toward the closest intersection S. 47th St and Westchester Ave. I looked in Greg's truck. He wasn't there. I looked in Juliet's car. She was not there. *Where's everyone?* I went to my house hoping they got my message. They weren't there either. Mom was fine. She was sitting at the dining room table working. *Phyllis where are you?* I looked in the laundry room and the kitchen. When I was in the kitchen, I saw Phyllis outside talking with Greg and Juliet. I immediately went to them. I was still invisible.

"Guys, I'm fine. They're holding me at 1534 S. 47th Street," I informed them.

Greg looked around, "Did ya'll hear that?"

Phyllis asked, "Brooke, are you here?"

"Yes. I can't stay long," I responded.

"We tracked your phone down. It was on the road, smashed," Greg informed me.

"They're holding me in the basement at 1534 S. 47th Street. I need to get back before they discover I'm gone," I said, about to leave.

"Brooke, are you sure this is the best thing to do? We can't protect you there," Greg said as I pulled out the mirror.

"Yes, we need to find a way to stop them, but to do that, I must pretend to be their captive," I explained.

Just as I was about to be sucked into the mirror, I heard Greg say, "I'll be hiding outside the house."

Before returning to the basement, I used the restroom in my room and grabbed a granola bar and my half-full bottle of water from my backpack. I hid my snack in a box in the corner before returning to my chains. I made myself comfortable on the floor with my back up against the wall. A bit of time passed before I took the hoody off. It was making me lightheaded. I felt myself drifting off. They awakened me when I heard them unlock the door. I stood up to make sure I was able to defend myself. They turned the light above me on. This felt blinding for a moment. I had been in the dark for so long. Eleni made her way toward me. Spiro was behind her at the top of the stairs. She kept a safe distance just at the edge of the light's glow. Even in the dim light, I could tell she was a beautiful woman.

She looked me over. "Spiro, I find it hard to believe you had a hard time with this girl. She's just a child," she said. Keeping her distance, she walked around, checking me out. Her head swayed as she gazed at me.

I kept my eye on her as she strolled around the room. I asked, "What do you want with me?"

She spoke, "Tell me what you know about the Bloom of Dreams."

I looked up in the air with an expression that said, what?

"Don't play stupid, child. I know you know what I'm talking about. Now tell me about the stone," she insisted.

"Eleni, I'm no child," I said sternly.

"That's yet to be determined," she said as she approached me.

I changed my stance to be able to kick her if she approached. She noticed and backed away. Eleni walked toward the stairs. She stopped and turned toward me, "Without a mirror, you're not going anywhere, my dear. You'll soon beg me to leave." Directing her attention to Spiro, "Don't feed her. She will give me that necklace without a battle or she will die of hunger." They exited the basement, shutting the light off before locking the door.

I released myself and teleported to spy on them upstairs. They were in the kitchen.

"Leave her here for a few days without food in the dark. She'll have a change of heart when we return. Come, you've done well. You can stay in my penthouse and enjoy the amenities. Let's get something to eat," she informed him. They headed out the front door. I moved next to the black Tesla in the driveway to get a look inside. I watched them drive off.

Using telepathy, I called out to Greg, "I'm on the front porch. Where are you?"

I heard some rustling in the bushes. Greg pushed through them and came to the front porch. "I'm so glad ya okay. I'll meet ya in my car," Greg said as he stepped off the porch and headed down the street.

I arrived at the truck and made myself visible. Greg hopped in and kissed me several times before saying, "I've been so worried about you." He leaned over and kissed me.

"I need to go home before my mother gets worried about me," I informed Greg.

Greg said, "Phyllis's covering for you. How about we get you some dinner?"

"It'll need to be something quick. Spiro and Eleni are eating out. I need to teleport to their car before they reach her place," I instructed. Greg drove us to Wendy's to get me something to eat. I filled him in on their plan to make me so weak I would not put up a fight. "I have not figured out how I'm going to be there and at school," I said, taking a bite of my spicy chicken sandwich.

Greg slurped his soda. He asked, "Can't ya use your power of persuasion to have them show up at night?"

"That's brilliant! I can make that work," I said, scarfing down the rest of my food. Anxiously waiting for Greg to finish his dinner.

Once Greg finished, I had him bring me home. I told Greg I would contact him after I found the location of Eleni's place.

I teleported to the Tesla and waited for them to leave the restaurant. Nearly thirty minutes later, they returned to the vehicle. They did not drive far. I followed them into the hotel and up to the Presidential Suite. The suite was like a very nice apartment. The main area had a large L-shaped sofa and a few chairs. The dining room was just behind the sofa. They sat down and began discussing me.

Eleni face seemed puzzled by something. She then said, "I don't understand why we can't just take the necklace. Why must she give it to us?"

"It's simple. Legend says they must give the stone to the recipient for it to have power. If we just take it, it will become useless," Spiro explained.

Is that true? I thought about it. It worked for me because my grandmother gave it to me. I gave it to Juliet, and it worked. She gave it back to me and it worked. I am going to need to test this theory.

"The day after tomorrow, we'll visit her. After breakfast, she should be more compliant," Eleni instructed.

Morning just won't work for me. I concentrated on persuading Spiro first, "Suggest waiting till evening."

Spiro said, "I think it would be better for us to stay away during the day. At night, fewer people would notice us."

Now I need to influence Eleni. I began using my power of persuasion on her. I concentrated on her mind and told her, "Spiro's right. It would be much safer at night."

Eleni got up and made herself a drink. She returned to Spiro. "Perhaps you are right. She should beg us for food by that time. I'm exhausted." She headed toward her bedroom.

There was nothing more for me to do here. I headed home.

BROOKE: I'm home.

GREG: Meet me in my truck.

I teleported to the truck and waited for him. Greg must have gone straight to the truck because I only waited a few seconds. He hopped in and handed me a red rose. It was fragrant. I thanked him.

He said, "Well, how did it go?"

"Your plan worked perfectly. They originally were going to come in the morning after breakfast, but I influenced them to come in the evening. They plan to stay away until the day after tomorrow."

"I'm glad it worked. I think we should be there with you. We don't know what they have planned to do to ya," Greg suggested.

"Spiro told Eleni the necklace will only work if I give it willingly. I don't know if that's true, but they believe it is," I said scooting over closer to him.

"That's interesting. I don't know how we could test that. Maybe the Bloom Keepers will think of something," Greg commented.

I placed my hand on Greg's hand, "Enough about that. How's your mom doing?"

Greg took his hand away and wrapped his arm around me, "I think yesterday was a bit much for her. She's been resting most of the day in her shed."

"I'm sorry to hear she's suffering. I will heal her, but I need to make sure she believes it's just part of her treatments," I said as I looked into his eyes. They started watering.

"Thank you," Greg hugged me tightly.

We held each other for a while. It was getting late. I needed to get some more homework done. Eleni and Spiro were interrupting my schedule. With people out to get me, I needed to stay ahead of my assignments. When I was too exhausted to keep my eyes open, I headed to bed.

Greg and I had our normal workout. He provided me with a new cell phone. He explained Phyllis helped him obtain it.

Our sparring matches were far more intense than they were when he first began training me. Greg was still superior in skill, but I was able to get a few good shots on him. I thought my skills were starting to surprise him. I showered and rode with Greg to school. In case they came by my house I did not want to take a chance at them seeing my car gone. We were having such a good time sparring; we were nearly late for class.

In the middle of my second class, my phone vibrated.

JULIET: Library 4:00 pm Room 2B

There was time to spare before the meeting. I found a quiet place in the library to study until it was time for us to meet. I packed up my books and headed toward the room. Bob and Sharon appeared to be studying together. The stone could do good things.

When I opened the door, it appeared they had started the meeting without me. They immediately stopped talking when I entered. Jacob started the meeting by saying, "We're here to discuss how to test the stone to see if it'll work when someone takes it from you. We've been discussing it and we could not come up with anything."

"I haven't been able to come up with anything myself," I added. Something told me they were not being completely honest with me. I filled everyone in on what had been going on with Spiro and Eleni. We discussed them being there invisible to assist me with whatever they had planned. Juliet was the only one who could not make it. We agreed to meet at the park and head over together.

That night, Mom, Phyllis, and I enjoyed a nice dinner. Mom informed us she was leaving in the morning on another trip. The three of us had a wonderful time. I went up to my room and saw I missed a call from Mechelle. I called her back immediately.

"I'm so glad you called back. There's a party this weekend. I wanted to see if you could go with me. I just met this girl. And she's going to be busy entertaining. The party's Saturday night," she said, almost pleading with me.

I knew she had not made many friends. I assured her I would be there. She sent me a picture of her room. I was to arrive at 8:00 pm.

Eleven

I went about my daily routine. Worked out with Greg, headed to class, studied, and had dinner with my family. Mom wanted to hang out with me after dinner. I informed her I had a study group to meet and needed to head out. I was about to leave when I realized I needed to be wearing the same outfit I had on when they put me in the basement. I ran up and started digging through my hamper, but the outfit was gone. I checked my closet. Phyllis had already washed it and put it away. With a quick clothing switch, I bolted to the park to meet the Bloom Keepers.

Everyone was there when I arrived. We didn't want to be seen doing it. We piled into Greg's truck because it had the darkest window tent. A scan of the area showed no one around. I teleported us all invisible. When we arrived, there was nothing to lead us to believe they had returned. "We are about to see if I can leave you invisible and become visible," I announced. I gazed into my mirror and teleported myself back to the same location, but this time I concentrated on me being visible, and them remaining invisible.

I didn't see anyone around the room. I asked, "Are you guys here?"

In perfect harmony, they all replied, "Yes."

"You need to roll around on the floor and make it appear you have been here a while," Juliet instructed.

We chatted for a few minutes to make sure everyone knew the plan. It was not long before we heard someone unlocking the basement door. I pretended to be asleep as I lay there handcuffed and shackled to the floor. I did not look up to see who it was. Using telepathy, I asked Jacob who was there. He told me it was Spiro and

81

Eleni. The light came on. I stirred a bit, trying to block the light from my eyes.

Eleni asked, "Brooke, are you ready to give me the Bloom of Dreams?" She walked closer to me. "Have you had enough? I bet you're hungry." She turned to Spiro and took a bag from him. Eleni put the bag on a table near her. She took something out of it. She moved closer, and said in a sweet voice, "I have a big juicy burger for you. Isn't that what you Americans love? You look so tired. This will give you some energy. All you have to do is give me the necklace, and it's yours."

Spiro got her a chair. She wasn't close enough for me to do anything. In a tired voice, I asked, "What's so special about this stone, anyway?"

"This stone belongs to my people. Echo's soul was placed in the stone. She needs to be put in her resting place. You don't have the power to do that," she explained.

I knew what she believed, but it had become a game to me. I knew the answer but asked anyway, "Echo?"

Spiro explained, "The god Pan fell in love with Echo. She did not want to have anything to do with Pan. He used his powers to panic the people. In their panic, they killed her. Her soul was placed in that stone. We just want Echo's soul to be at peace."

I sat up. "Really. What makes you think this is the stone?"

"Greek mythology has described the stone. Have you ever seen another one like yours? I assure you, yours is one of a kind," Spiro informed me.

"This was a gift from my grandmother. I'm not parting with it, no matter what you say," I said sternly.

Eleni turned to Spiro and asked him to get her bag. She turned her attention back to me. "I wanted to do this the easy way. You think you being here was hard. It's about to become a lot harder for you, Brooke. One way or another, you'll give me that stone."

"You'll have to take it off my cold, dead body before you'll be able to get it from me," I snarled.

"We can arrange that," she said. Spiro returned with her bag. She pulled out a taser and a small case. She opened the case on the floor. It appeared to be some torture device.

Sarcastically I asked, "Is Zeus your god?"

Eleni stood up and sternly said, "Hellenism is no joking matter."

"Please forgive me. I didn't mean to offend you. Jesus is my Lord and savior. As a child of God, I must warn you. He's got my back," I said as I stood up to show her. I was not weak at all.

She grabbed her taser and approached me. When something knocked it out of her hand. Eleni looked confused as she recovered from the attack. I used telepathy to find out who did this. Juliet admitted it was her.

"What's the matter, Eleni? I told you I wouldn't give it to you. Perhaps you should try to take it. Come on, I dare you," I said, wanting to come out of these chains. We thought it best not to show her I could easily go through things.

Spiro came after me with a metal chair. He tripped and found himself at my feet. I kicked him in the stomach. He curled up and groaned for a moment. Spiro finally retreated.

"Perhaps you should stay down here until you die," Eleni threatened.

I felt something on my leg. The shackle released its hold on me. Eleni and Spiro's mouths fell open. I pulled my hands out of the handcuffs and they dropped to the floor behind my back. They clanked on the floor. The sound immediately drew their eyes to them. "You better run," I said as I started moving toward them. Eleni took off and ran into one of the Bloom Keepers. She recovered from her near fall and appeared confused at what had happened. They both bolted up the stairs and out of the basement. It was only seconds when I heard a car squeal out of the driveway.

Each of us burst out laughing. It was weird not being able to see them. I went to teleport us back to Greg's truck, and Jacob stopped me because he was not holding on yet. When I felt each of them on my arm, I took us back to Greg's truck, making us visible.

Juliet said to Jacob, "It was so funny when she ran into you."

I notice Jacob had the burger in his lap. I rolled my eyes and sarcastically said, "Seriously?"

He looked up and smiled. "There's no need to waste a perfectly good burger," Jacob said, grabbing the burger. He was just about to bite into it when Greg offered his opinion. "They may have poisoned it."

Jacob dropped it back in the box and got out of the truck to throw it away. As he was about to get back in, the police pulled up behind us. Jacob got in and quickly buckled up.

The officer tapped on Greg's window. Greg rolled it down. "Is everything okay, sir?"

He moved his flashlight across each of our faces. 'I don't think I've seen you here before. Are you aware the park's closed?"

"No. Sorry. We were just leaving," Greg said politely.

"The park closes at sunset. I was just coming back to write you a ticket, but since you are leaving, have a pleasant night," he said. He turned his lights off and moved on.

Each of us got into our own vehicles and headed home. I realized as I thought about the event. Eleni may have been a little spooked by what happened, but I got the feeling I had not seen the last of her or Spiro.

I entered through the back door. I was hoping not to run into Phyllis, but I was not so lucky. She looked me over. "You're filthy," she said, grabbed my sleeve. "I just washed this."

"I'm sorry Phyllis. I'll explain another time. I need to get showered." I headed upstairs to get cleaned up. After drying my hair, I noticed I missed a call from Greg and Juliet. I called Juliet back first.

"We didn't get the chance to tell you, but you were amazing tonight. You stood your ground with her. It was quite impressive. I know you couldn't see it but with every comment you made, our faces showed we were all surprised by your strength to keep her in line. Jacob's was the funniest. His eyes got so big when you told her about Jesus. We're all very proud of you," Juliet flattered me.

I told her I loved Eleni's face when she pushed the taser out of her hand. She explained she kicked it away from her. We talked for a few minutes longer. I curled up in my bed and called Greg back.

Greg had forgotten his mother's surgery was the next day. He wanted to spend time with her before she went to bed. He also told me he was proud of me. I asked him if I could visit her in the hospital the next day. He thought it best to wait and see her when she was home. I told him I loved him, and I would pray for her, which I did. *How can I heal her without it being so apparent a miracle occurred?* I felt it best to wait until she was about to be checked to make sure her cancer was gone.

I woke up thinking about Joann. I went out onto my balcony to see if they had left yet. Andrew's car was gone. I said a quick prayer for her before texting Greg.

| **BROOKE:** | Are you heading to the hospital? |

| **GREG:** | No. Mom wanted me to go to school. I'm not up for a workout. |

| **BROOKE:** | Do you want to come over for breakfast? I'm heading down now. |

| **GREG:** | Sure. |

Phyllis was sitting at the counter drinking her tea and reading her bible when I snuck up on her. I told her about Joann and explained Greg would join us for breakfast. She got up, and I told her I would cook. There weren't many things I cooked, but I made good egg sandwiches. I looked all over the refrigerator for bacon but could not find any. "Where's the bacon?"

"We are out. There's sausage," Phyllis informed me. Greg knocked on the back door, and Phyllis let him in. They chatted while I cooked. I saw she had croissants out. This inspired me to make sausage, egg and cheese, sandwich on a croissant.

We ate at the counter. Greg told Phyllis his mother should be home from the hospital tomorrow. She told him she would bring dinner over for them, so they did not need to worry about anything but taking care of her. She was fond of Greg's family.

I tried to keep Greg from worrying about his mother. We met up for a few minutes after our first class. Midway through my second class, he texted.

| **GREG:** | Dad texted. Mom did well. She's in recovery. |

| **BROOKE:** | Praise God. I love you. |

Greg spent the evening at the hospital with his family. I spent the night studying for a test the next day.

The next day, I rushed home after class to help Phyllis make them dinner. It was a lot to make meals for two families. I learned how to make a chicken pot pie from scratch. We made two large ones. She had me take it over, but I insisted she come with me. Joann was in her room when we arrived. Greg told us she wanted us to go in and see her. I got a good look at her bedroom while she thanked us for the sweet gesture.

Friday, we had a Bloom Keepers meeting. Jacob informed us Eleni and Spiro were still in Kentucky. He had not figured out what their plan was but would continue working on it. I told them about my plans to spend Saturday night with Mechelle. I did not want them to worry about me. Greg seemed happy I would not be around. He agreed. Eleni was not finished with me yet. Juliet told me to tell my mother I was hanging out with her for the evening so she would not get suspicious about why I would be out so late. I hated lying to her. Jacob and Juliet stayed in the library to study. Greg walked me to my car. He had errands to run and would be helping his mother with the house. We spent a few minutes chatting and said our goodbyes before I headed home.

Before heading to bed, I texted Mechelle.

BROOKE: How about I come over early, and we get ready together.

MECHELLE: Definitely!! How about 6:00 pm.

BROOKE: Sounds good. I can't wait to see you!

Twelve

Greg and I went to Cherokee Park for our workout and to make a day of it. We brought small backpacks with water bottles, sandwiches, and a couple of apples. The park was beautiful with a creek winding through it and trees canopying the area. Very different from anything we had in South Florida. We parked near a hiking path entrance and stretched before entering the path. The terrain was rough in some areas, with roots from the trees. I discovered the roots by accident. The sunlight was shining through the leaves. I found it incredibly peaceful until I fell face-first to the ground. I lifted my face and began spitting dirt out of my mouth.

Greg must have heard me because he came to help me get up. My knee was bleeding a bit, and he said I scratched my face. He took off his backpack and pulled out a small first aid kit. I moved off the path to let another group of hikers pass us. I laid down to admire the sun peering through the trees, while Greg tended to my knee. The stone heated. I lifted my head up and looked around.

"Um, Brooke," he said, pointing to my knee. "You're healing right before my eyes."

I sat up and watched my body heal. Surprised, I said, "Wow! That's cool!"

Greg pointed to my face and said, "It's like it never happened." He leaned in for a better look. I watched him as he checked it out. Once he made eye contact with me. I leaned in for a kiss.

Greg helped me up. We continued our hike. I kept an eye on the terrain. As we jogged down the path, we came across a fallen tree. We leaped over it and continued our hike. We came out into a clearing. Perched on a tree was a Red-Tailed Hawk. I stopped dead in my tracks to observe its beauty.

Greg asked, "Ya okay?"

"Yes, look," I said, pointing to the hawk. Turning my attention to the hawk, I asked it, "Please come down so I can get a better look at you."

The hawk tilted its head and turned its body to face me.

"It's like he understands ya," Greg commented.

I asked the hawk again, but this time using telepathy. The hawk left his perch and landed about eight feet from me. I bowed and thanked him. Greg's eyes moved from me to the bird. I glanced over and he seemed amazed. The bird looked at both of us and flew off.

When we were not within earshot of anyone, we discussed all the amazing things the stone permitted me to do. Greg confessed he was jealous he had not had an opportunity to use the stone. He reminded me that both Juliet and Jacob have been able to experience it.

I must admit, it had not occurred to me. I assured him he could use it soon. We continued hiking until we found a picnic area to eat at.

As I watched him eat, I tried to think of a way that would be special for him to use the stone. Perhaps he could take us on our next date, or I could let him talk with the next animal we come across.

Greg answered his phone, "Yes, ma'am. I love you too." He returned his phone to his pocket and explained, "Karen's spending the night at a friend's house tonight. Mom wants me to drop her off when I get home."

I asked about his mother. Greg explained she was sleeping a lot. That was when it hit me. *I've got a surprise for you.* I knew how he should use the stone. It was tough to figure out when he should use the stone, but I had decided. It was important I keep my surprise for him to myself until the day came. I was going to let him use it.

Greg and I said our goodbyes in his driveway. I was going to shower and relax for the rest of the day. I suspected I would be out late.

I must have dozed off. Thankfully, I was not late for meeting Mechelle. Mom was not home, so I could leave my room. I brought my makeup bag and a couple of outfits for Mechelle to determine what was best for this party. I looked through the mirror and saw her laying on her bed. Mechelle seemed startled when I stepped through the mirror into her room. She leaped off her bed. She grabbed me by the shoulders and said, "Holly cannoli, you scared me!"

I apologized and laid my clothes on her bed. Mechelle and I did each other's makeup. She loved both outfits I brought. She wore one, and I wore the other. It was like old times. Mechelle drove us to the party, which was close to the college.

There were a few cars outside. Mechelle rang the doorbell and waited for someone to answer. A stunning girl with long blond wavy hair and glasses answered the door, "Mechelle, I'm so glad you came." She turned to me and said, "You must be Brooke. I'm Miranda. Come on in." She shut the door and hollered into the other room, "Katie!" A brunette came into view with a big smile. "Katie, this is Mechelle and Brooke. Would you get them something to drink?"

Katie smiled and led us to the kitchen. There were sodas, orange juice, and cranberry juice, along with various types of alcohol to choose from. "Help yourself to whatever you would like. There's ice in that cooler," Katie said, pointing to a red cooler in the corner of the room.

Mechelle and I both grabbed a sprite and found a seat in the living room. Miranda seemed busy with hostess things. We took this time to discuss our summer vacation. Mechelle wanted to get to know my friends in Kentucky. Being she was single now; I think she might have been interested in seeing Austin again. Austin did not know my secret, but I was certain we could easily keep him from finding out. We decided I would bring her to one of our Bloom Keeper meetings, and we could discuss options for the summer.

The house was packed with college students. We went to the kitchen and waited in line to grab some food. Two guys approached us. They seemed a little intoxicated. They began flirting with us. I politely explained we were taken. The taller of the two did not seem to care. Mechelle seemed to like the attention she was getting from the shorter, more sober one. I did not want to leave her alone, but I needed a restroom. She assured me she was fine and would wait for me.

There was a line for the restroom. It had been about fifteen minutes before it was my turn. The bathroom was a disaster. Miranda's home was so clean when we arrived. I picked up some of the trash from the floor. The wastebasket was nearly full. I washed my hands and made my way back to Mechelle. She was nowhere in sight. I scanned the common areas of the house. *Where are you, Mechelle?* I felt like I could not breathe. I needed to find her.

Using telepathy, I called out to her, "Mechelle, where are you?"

"Brooke, help me. I'm in a bedroom upstairs," Mechelle told me. She sounded in distress. I bolted up the stairs. I looked down the hall of closed doors. *Which one?* I opened the first one. It was empty. The second one had two girls fixing their makeup in front of a dresser. The next door was locked. I banged on the door, "Mechelle." She did not call back to me. I was ready to break the door down when I heard Mechelle in my head say, "He's covering my mouth. You're at the door."

I reached through the door and unlocked it. I slammed the door open; Mechelle was on the bed, being held down by the guy she had been talking with.

He looked up and smiled. "Are you wanting to join us?"

The door shut. It was the tall guy holding his cell phone. It seemed like he was recording.

"Brooke, I think he put something in my drink," Mechelle said in a groggy voice.

The tall guy grabbed me and tried to get me to the floor. I grabbed him and flipped him over onto his back. I pulled the short guy off Mechelle. It looked like I was able to rescue her before anything serious happened. The little guy started jumping around like he was going to hit me. Unexpectedly, the tall guy grabbed me from behind. The door flung open. Miranda and Katie stood there with their mouths wide open. I kicked the little guy, and he flung up against the wall. I stomped on the tall guy's foot and jabbed him with my elbow. He released his grip. I punched him across his jaw.

Two guys came in and took them out of the room. Miranda was at Mechelle's side. She apologized. She did not know them. They had come with another guest. Miranda wanted to call the police.

Mechelle looked at me and said, "No. I'm fine. I just need a minute."

"Take as long as you need," Miranda said. She shut the door on her way out.

"He must have put something in my drink," she said worried and in a slurred voice.

I hugged her and felt the stone heating.

"Brooke, I feel warm all over," she said, squeezing me tighter.

The stone returned to its normal temperature. I pulled away from her and said, "How do you feel now?"

She looked confused. "I feel fine now. Thank you." She hugged me again.

When Mechelle was ready, we headed downstairs. Katie and Miranda met up with us. Miranda confirmed with Mechelle she was okay. She was more than willing to contact the police. I think she knew she could get in trouble, but she seemed more concerned about Mechelle than herself.

Katie turned to me. "You are amazing. Did you know you just beat the crap out of two guys?"

I smiled, not knowing how to respond. Mechelle and Miranda hung out for a while and seemed to bond. Mechelle started having a good time. We decided to leave at a decent hour. Mechelle gave me my outfit back before I headed home.

I had several missed calls from Greg. I changed before calling him back, "I saw you called a few times. Is everything okay?"

"Eleni's parked down the street. She's been watching your house. I saw the Tesla when I took Karen over to her friend's house," he said.

I asked, "Do you know if they are still there?"

"She left about an hour ago. Don't let your guard down," he advised. He asked about my time with Mechelle. He was not happy to hear about what had occurred, but he was glad I was able to prevent anything from happening. Once we were both caught up on the evening's events, we said good night.

I made myself invisible and teleported to the front yard to confirm she was no longer there. She was nowhere in sight. I returned to my room. I spent the rest of the night going through my social media until I was tired enough to head to bed.

The next morning, I called Mechelle to see how she was doing. She was much better. Miranda and she had already spoken today about the incident. Apparently, the two guys did not know anyone at the party. Mechelle explained, "I had heard about people putting drugs in people's drinks, but I never suspected it would happen to me. I can't thank you enough for coming to my rescue. After the event, I might reconsider working out with you."

"That would be nice, but I think I would have a hard time explaining how you magically appeared here every day," I said with a chuckle.

Mechelle explained, "Miranda, Katie, and I are going to take some self-defense classes together."

I explained that if she pressed charges against the boys, it would be difficult for me to explain my presence. She understood. Mechelle said she was worried about getting Miranda in trouble also. Miranda had proclaimed she would not be having any more parties. Despite what had happened, Mechelle seemed to handle the situation well.

I headed down for breakfast. A group text came in.

JULIET: Meeting at 1:30 pm at Brooke's house.

Why would she be having it at my house? Mom was sitting at the table drinking her coffee. I greeted her and continued to the kitchen to get myself a cup. Phyllis was pulling a breakfast casserole out of the oven. She turned to me. "Good morning. Did you sleep well?"

I added cream and sugar to my coffee. "I did. Thanks. You seem to be in an exceptionally good mood today. What's up?"

"I was up early taking care of some business for our meeting later," Phyllis said suspiciously.

I whispered, "How come everyone seems to know about this meeting but me? And why are we having it here?"

She whispered back, "Your mom's taking a separate car to church. She and Lance have a date."

I gave her a look that said; I know you're up to something. My mother and I sat in the dining room together. Phyllis was behind me with the casserole.

We had a nice breakfast, but I stayed chatting a little too long. I rushed up and showered for church. As I washed my neck, I suddenly realized my necklace was gone. *Think I had it with Mechelle, or I would not have made it home. I had it when I went to bed.* Someone must have taken it off me when I was sleeping. I jumped out of the shower and called Phyllis. "It's gone! Someone took the necklace off me while I slept."

Phyllis giggled, "Stop panicking. I have it. Now, get dressed." The line went dead. She did not even explain why she had it. I barely dried my hair because I wanted to know what was going on. Once dressed, I found Phyllis. She explained I could have it back at the meeting.

I sat through church wondering why she would just take it. She should know if she needed it for something I would have loaned it to her. I rode home with Phyllis. She would not tell me anything. I changed before everyone arrived and went downstairs to help Phyllis.

I was annoyed and didn't want to, but I knew it was the right thing to do.

Once the Bloom Keepers were in the dining room, I wanted to start the meeting. Everyone insisted we start after lunch. *What's going on?* I watched everyone eat, and they seemed to know some joke I knew nothing about. By this point, I was beyond irritated.

Once the table was cleared, Phyllis started the meeting. "Brooke, we had a secret meeting without you to determine if the stone worked, if I took it from you. You had given permission for Jacob and Juliet to use the stone, so we thought it best they do not try to take it. It would not be appropriate for Greg and Jacob to be in your room at night. They asked me to take it from you. Early this morning, I snuck into your room and took the Bloom of Dreams without you even noticing. I have the answer to the abilities of the stone if someone takes it." She pulled her blouse down enough for us to see she had the necklace on. Juliet handed her a small mirror. She focused on the mirror and was sucked into it. She returned immediately.

I sat there, not knowing what to say.

Phyllis handed Juliet her mirror and took the necklace off and placed it around her neck. "I must admit, I have had a fun morning playing with this. I checked in on my sister and visited my parent's graves."

We discussed Eleni watching my house. We knew she was not out of the picture, but everyone needed to be careful. They seem to know a lot about me, including who my friends are. I explained she might have someone watching them as well. Following our brief meeting, we enjoyed a cherry pie and played board games before everyone headed home.

Thirteen

Days later, Jacob requested a meeting. I contacted Mechelle, and she could attend this meeting. I picked her up from her dorm and took her to a restroom in our University of Louisville's library. She was grateful. We arrived at the handicap stall. She was picturing her foot winding up in the toilet. She was impressed with the library. On the way to the room, I ran into Tammy. I had not seen her since we took our tour. She was happy to know I had settled in well.

Everyone was glad to see Mechelle when she walked through the door to our reserved room. Once the door shut, Jacob called the meeting to order, "Eleni has returned to Greece, but Spiro's still here. I have seen him around campus a few times."

Greg interrupted, "Brooke and I've seen him on our street."

Jacob continued, "I'm not sure when they'll make a move on you, Brooke. I think we need to be prepared no matter what they've planned."

"I'm glad they don't know the full power of the stone. That's given us an advantage. We need to deter them from ever coming after it. Perhaps you and Juliet can find something we can use to deter them," I responded to Jacob. No one had anything additional to add regarding Eleni and Spiro. "As you know, I invited Mechelle to our meeting. She's an honorary member. She and I have been discussing summer break. Mechelle would like to get to know everyone better and we thought it would be great to plan a summer trip. Perhaps for a week. What do you guys think?"

"I know Greg loved being in the tropical climate. I thought perhaps Jamaica or the Bahamas," Mechelle suggested.

"That sounds good, or we could go to Hawaii. I could show everyone around," Juliet added.

Jacob chimed in, "It depends on the cost. I make some money working on people's computers, but I don't think I could afford anything that extravagant."

"I'm with Jacob. I would love to do a big trip, but I think it would need to be something less expensive," I commented.

"My grandma has a beach house on Myrtle Beach. I will see if she will let us come there for a week. She's usually gone on a cruise part of the summer. We would just need to keep it clean and pay for our own food," Mechelle offered an alternative.

"It should take us about eight hours to get there," Jacob commented.

Mechelle explained she would fly up and meet us there. She told us she would talk to her grandmother this week. She also explained we would need to bring a car. Her grandmother does not keep a spare one at the home.

We concluded the meeting. Greg asked if we wanted to grab a pizza before I took Mechelle back to her door. Mechelle seemed happy with that. Everyone headed to the pizza parlor in their own vehicles. Mechelle rode with me.

It was nice being able to hang out with Mechelle more. I had really missed her. Greg arrived first and got us a table. Juliet and Jacob strolled in after Mechelle and I. Mechelle asked Jacob, "Do you carry your computer with you everywhere?"

Juliet laughed, "Pretty much." She leaned over and kissed him. Jacob explained he did a lot of side work repairing computers and he got calls all the time. He made decent money at it because he was always available and willing to work when they need help.

We ordered drinks. I heard the bell on the door ring to notify the staff of a new customer entering the establishment. I looked up and saw the surprise Greg and I had for Mechelle. Austin walked up and said, "Hey guys."

Mechelle looked up. Her eyes widened as soon as she saw Austin. He laid his hand on her shoulder. "I'm glad they told me you were in town."

Austin joined us and we witnessed a little flirting going on between Mechelle and Austin. Jacob scarfed down a few pieces of the pie and announced he had to leave. He kissed Juliet goodbye and headed out. Just after he left the stone started heating. I looked around the restaurant. No one had walked in. I looked outside. Jacob was being approached by a man. I looked closer. It was Spiro. Using telepathy, I told Greg and asked him to stay with Austin & Mechelle. "Juliet and I'll be right back."

Juliet looked confused but followed me. She whispered, "What's your hurry?"

The minute the door opened, I noticed Jacob put his computer on top of his car. He leaned over and thrust his leg into Spiro's chest. I started running toward Jacob. It sounded like Juliet was right behind me. Spiro came after him again. He had something in his hand. Jacob punched him across the jaw. Spiro shook it off. He looked over at us and ran to a nearby vehicle and left.

Juliet hugged Jacob. "Are you okay?"

Jacob shook his hand, and said, "Other than my fist, I'm fantastic! Did you see my moves?"

Juliet and I smiled.

"You did well. You should be proud of yourself." He seemed to be going after my friends now. "Everyone needs to be careful. I want everyone to check in every day. We need to make sure everyone is okay and accounted for," I insisted.

"Look, I gotta go," he kissed Juliet again. We watched him pull out and did not see anyone attempt to follow him. Juliet and I headed back to the restaurant. Using telepathy, I told Greg what had happened. When we returned to the table, Mechelle seemed to know something was up but said nothing. When we were ready to leave. Greg and I went to his truck to say goodbye, and Austin and Mechelle went to my car. Juliet headed home. I explained how fantastic Jacob was with Spiro. We kissed a few times before he announced he was heading out and said goodbye to Mechelle.

As soon as we were in the car, Mechelle said, "Thank you for inviting him." She buckled up with a smile on her face as she watched him walk to his truck. When we pulled out, she asked, "What happened? Why did you and Juliet leave the restaurant so abruptly?"

I filled her in. Once I was near my home, I asked her to duck down in the car. I pulled into my driveway and parked by the garage. We spoke a few more minutes before I pulled out my mirror and asked her to hold on. I teleported us back to her dorm. She fell to the ground and looked up at me. "That was an awkward landing."

We both laughed. I told her I needed to get back. We said our goodbyes. I teleported back to my car before heading into the house.

Mom was in the sitting room talking to someone on the phone. I waved as I headed up to my room. When I got to the second-floor landing, I noticed Phyllis was in the library reading. I knocked on the door frame. "How was your day?"

Phyllis leaned her book against her chest. "Pretty uneventful. The cleaning lady your mother hired to help me was here today, which means I have had time to relax some. How was your day?"

I closed the door and sat down next to her. "For the most part, it was pretty good. Spiro attacked Jacob tonight, just after he left us. He did a great job defending himself. I'm worried about them going after you and Mom. Jacob and Juliet are trying to find something we could use to deter them."

"I've known for a long time being here and knowing what I know makes me a target. It wasn't always that way. Your grandmother hired me to cook and clean for her. Neither of us knew we would become so close or that she would share her secret with me. She and I had become friends and she asked me to join her on a trip. She wanted to do something nice for me. We went to New York for a few days. We both wanted to see the Macy's Thanksgiving Day Parade. That trip, she used the stone to save us from Anthony Granaldi III."

She leaned over and put her bookmark in her book and placed it on the table. She continued, "Anthony was much younger. I'll never forget that night. It was about 10:30 pm. We had gone to see Cats. It had been raining, but the rain had stopped. We went into the alley to cut over to the next street. We didn't know Anthony had been following us. He caught up to us in the alley and confronted your mother at gunpoint. He wanted the necklace. Lillie managed to get the gun out of his hand. They fought for a few minutes. She knocked him down and she ran in my direction. She grabbed my hand. We ran straight for a large puddle. The next thing I knew, we were in our hotel suite. That was the night Lillie told me about the Bloom of Dreams."

"I think about her a lot. I wish she had told me about the stone and her many adventures," I said.

"Lillie would be very proud of you. She was certain you were the only person she felt could handle the responsibility. You know you are going to need to pick someone to replace you," she advised.

"Phyllis, I'm not planning on having children anytime soon," I explained.

Phyllis giggled, "I hope not. I know Lillie would want this responsibility to remain within the family, but I don't know if there's anyone that could handle it."

I thought about who I would trust to protect the stone. "I would have thought Kevin, but him not being able to cope well with his recent encounter tells me he would not be a good fit. Perhaps Allison," I responded.

Phyllis asked, "Allison might be a good person for the short term. Is there anyone outside the family you would consider?"

"Sure, Greg or Juliet would be great candidates. If Jacob improves his skills, he would be good also," I stated.

Phyllis smiled, "I agree. You have a great team working with you. I think you should speak with Mr. Thomas about setting up a will for yourself."

Phyllis made a good point. I needed to look into it. We chatted for a few more minutes and then I retired to my room to work on my assignments.

Fourteen

James and I met up in one of the rooms at the library. We had reserved it to finalize the final touches of our presentation for our class. We had the room until the Bloom Keepers meeting at 4:00 pm. Our presentation was on how bullying affects one's development. We did a skit to show how it can affect someone. James wanted to be the bully. That humored me because he was a sweetheart. We practiced our skit over and over. It was only ten minutes long, but we wanted it to be perfect. James was really in his character. He grabbed my backpack from my arm and threw it on the ground. "Dork, no matter how hard you try, no one wants to be around you. You're ugly and stupid," James said as he gently pushed me. I acted cowardly.

We had not seen Greg come in. Greg puffed up his chest and aggressively approached James. "Man, what do you think you're doing?" Greg got in James's face. He was fuming.

"Chill man. It's not what you think," James tried to defuse the situation.

I jumped between them and quickly explained to Greg what was going on. I asked if he wanted to see our entire presentation.

"No, thanks. I think you guys nailed it. I'm sorry, man. I shouldn't have jumped to conclusions," Greg said, sounding embarrassed.

"No worries," James said, packing his things up. "I guess we're ready."

"I think so. If you want to meet before class to run through it one more time before our presentation, let me know," I said as I packed up my things.

"Well, that was humiliating," Greg said as he put his arms around my waist and kissed me.

"I've never seen you so mad," I laughed. We kissed again and were interrupted by Jacob and Juliet.

Everyone sat down. Jacob informed us of his latest discoveries by saying, "Eleni has a daughter. She has kept her out of the spotlight, but I found her. She's attending a boarding school in Switzerland." He showed us a picture of a teenage girl with dark hair. "Zahara's fourteen and loves fencing and horseback riding. We were not able to get her schedule," he added.

Juliet chimed in, "We were thinking you get some photos of her and threaten to kidnap her or something."

"I hope threatening her will be enough. I hate to say it, but we may need to take her," Greg added.

Jacob handed me a piece of paper. He pointed at the paper and said, "I wrote the information for a Polaroid camera. Do you think Leonardo could get it?"

"I hope it doesn't come to that. I guess I am going to head to Switzerland," I concluded.

Juliet shot me a look of excitement at me. She said, "I think this might be a two-person job." She smiled and batted her eyes at me.

I put my palm on her head and gently pushed her away while rolling my eyes. I grabbed my phone to see how many hours ahead of us Switzerland was. *Six hours.* "I'll see what Leonardo can do for me regarding a camera. I'll head over in the morning once I have the camera," I informed them.

We concluded our meeting. Jacob and Juliet had work to do in the library. Greg walked me to my car. I was nearly home when I heard my phone buzz. At the light, I checked to see who contacted me.

PHYLLIS: On your way home, please pick up creamer for coffee.

I informed her I would. Honk, Honk. I looked up. The light changed. I preceded to the grocery store and picked up my creamer. The closer I got to my vehicle, the warmer the stone became. I scanned the area for a sign of Eleni or Spiro. I did not see them. I was nearly to my car when Spiro jumped out in front of me.

"Walk that way," he said with his hand in his pocket.

It appeared he might have had a gun pointing at me. I walked in the direction he pointed. I looked back at him.

102

"Keep moving," he instructed, pushing me in the back with what felt like it might be a gun.

A man who appeared to be in his thirties must have noticed Spiro pushing me. He came up to me and gave me a hug. He said boisterously, "I haven't seen you in so long." The man whispered in my ear, "Are you okay?"

The last thing I wanted was for this stranger to get hurt. I calmly said, "Thank you for your concern. I'll be fine."

He turned to Spiro and asked, "Who's your friend? I don't think we've met. I'm Robert." He reached his hand out to shake Spiro's hand.

Spiro looked confused. He pulled his hand out of his pocket to shake the man's hand. Robert gripped it and pulled Spiro to him. "It appears you're up to something and I would hate for something to happen to you. I suggest you leave," he said, turning to me. "You can leave now. This gentleman and I are going to let you head home."

Spiro tried to pull his arm back, but the man appeared to be winning. I ran back to my car and scrunched down to return to Robert and Spiro invisible.

"You don't know who you are messing with," Spiro told Robert.

I reached into his pocket. The metal was cold to the touch. I grabbed the gun and returned to my vehicle. Without hesitation, I drove off. I shoved the gun under my front seat. I drove extra cautiously to avoid any chance of getting pulled over.

When I got home, I slipped the gun into my backpack, dropped off the creamer, then headed to my room.

BROOKE: I need your help ASAP

GREG: I'm helping my mom. Be over when done.

I sat on my bed staring at my backpack, wondering what to do with the weapon I now have in my possession. *Will he report it stolen? Was it used for other crimes?* I began pacing the room. Thinking about what I should do. My mind was racing. *Hurry Greg.* While I waited, I put my phone on my dresser and headed to see Leonardo. I looked around. It was late. I headed to his room.

Isabella answered the door and pulled me inside. She looked me over and said, "You're here late. Is everything okay?"

I handed her the note with the details about the Polaroid camera I needed. I expressed the urgency of needing this. She asked me to check back tomorrow afternoon. He should be able to get it easily. I returned to my room, grabbed my phone, and headed downstairs. I did not want to touch the gun, which meant doing my studying was out of the question. Phyllis was in the sitting room reading. "I figured you would be cooking. I was going to help," I said to her.

"Your mother wanted Chinese. She should be home in an hour or so," Phyllis informed me.

I explained my dilemma with the gun to her.

She suggested, "Wipe the prints off the gun and drop it off at the police station in Greece. They'll never suspect you because you have not left the country and have been attending class. You have an alibi, even if he reports it stolen. How will he be able to explain it getting stolen here and being returned there just hours later?"

I kissed her on the cheek. "You're brilliant!" I ran upstairs to find some pictures of the police station in Athens, Greece.

I could not find pictures of the inside.

GREG: I'm on my way.

I ran down to let him in. On the way to the library, I filled him in on the plan and what had happened. Greg said he would go with me. He also cleaned the gun and wrapped it in a towel to bring with us. Greg ran home to change and met me in my garage.

We arrived in front of the station. It was a three-story building. There were two officers out front talking. We waited for them to move away from the door before entering. There were too many people in the area to leave the gun. Someone might notice it suddenly appear when we leave. We walked down a hall and saw some offices. One door had an Evidence Room sign posted on the front of it. I moved through the door when Greg stopped me. We talked using telepathy.

Greg asked, "Where are we going?"

I explained we were heading into the Evidence Room. This is the perfect place for the gun to be discovered. We moved through the door. A lady was working at the counter in what looked like a cage. Greg and I moved through the wall and headed to the back area. There was a counter along the left wall with a man going through a box and writing on a form. We waited a minute. He placed the lid on the box and carried it to some shelves on the other side of the room.

Greg pulled the gun out of his bag. We had already wiped it clean of all fingerprints before we wrapped it up. He unrolled the gun and placed it on the counter. He was careful not to let his hands touch the weapon. As soon as it was on the counter, I grabbed his arm and brought him back to the garage. We stood inside talking for a few minutes. The garage door clicked on and started opening.

"Mom's home," I announced.

He looked at me and asked, "Won't she think it's weird we are hanging out in the garage?"

I did not have time to respond. We moved out of her way to allow her to get the car in the garage. Once she parked, I opened her car door. I did not give her a chance to speak. "We are here to help you carry the food in."

"Isn't that sweet," she said, handing each of us a bag. Mom held the door open for us. We took everything to the kitchen counter. Mom thanked us and headed toward the foyer. She had a habit of taking her heels off and leaving them on the step to take upstairs. As soon as she left the room. I gave Phyllis a thumbs up to let her know the gun was gone.

Greg joined us for dinner. We helped clear the table once the meal was over. Greg and I headed to the library. I shut the door and told him I would be right back. I went to the villa to get the Polaroid camera from Leonardo. He was nowhere to be found, but Isabella had the camera behind the check-in counter. I grabbed it and apologized for needing to leave in a hurry.

When we returned, we worked on my trip to Switzerland. Greg felt it would be good if Juliet joined me. The school was six stories and only had 75 students. We could cover more ground trying to find Zahara. Juliet would be over in the morning after my mother headed to work. As hard as we tried, Greg and I could not find a floor plan for the school. We were confident in the plan to track her down. I walked Greg to the front porch, and we said goodnight to each other.

Fifteen

Juliet arrived a few minutes before 8:00 am. It was 2:00 pm in Switzerland. I had the camera ready to go. Juliet seemed extremely excited to be heading abroad. We both took a good look at the photo we had of her before we made our way to the front door of the school. To the right was a receptionist and just past her desk was a wall of clocks for different time zones. Juliet and I were to speak using telepathy. I had the camera. Just past the reception area was a library. There were only a few girls there studying. None appeared to be Zahara. At the end of the hall was the dining hall. There was no one there either. I heard voices from the other side of the cafeteria. I looked in and saw an art class. Juliet and I looked around and did not see Zahara. Five more floors to go.

Juliet stopped me as I started heading upstairs. She pointed at a schedule on the wall. It appeared there were classrooms on the 5th floor. We peaked into the science class. There was a girl on the far side of the room that might possibly be her. She had her hair covering a portion of her face and we could not be certain. Knowing she should be in the room for a while we moved on to the other classrooms. Just down the hall was the English classroom. The students were studying the characters in Little Women.

We checked out the next room. The girls were learning etiquette. I found this class remarkably interesting. They were discussing the proper use of utensils. The instructor was explaining the appropriate way to hold a fish knife. She went on to explain how the United States was one of the few cultures where a knife is in the right hand to cut. We place the knife at the top of our plate and switch our fork to our right hand. In European dining, they eat with their fork in their left hand and their wrists rest on the edge of the table. As I listened to the differences in the cultures. I looked over at Juliet,

"Yikes. I'm doing this all wrong." She looked as if she was holding back a laugh. Juliet motioned for me to leave the room.

We returned to the science classroom. At this point, we were certain Zahara was the girl on the other side of the room. She was sitting up and listening to her instructor. There was not a lot of room to walk around. We waited quietly next to the door. We noticed some of the girls putting their supplies away. I pulled Juliet into the hall. "The hallways are narrow, and it's going to be difficult to stay out of everyone's way and follow her. Head down to the third floor, I'll stay on the fourth floor. We need to follow her," Juliet and I headed to our locations. It appeared the classes might be over for the day. It seemed everyone from the fifth floor was making their way downstairs. Some of the girls headed down the fourth-floor hallway and into what I presume were their dorms. Others continued down the stairwell. A large group was coming straight for me. I had sunk into the wall to avoid being run over. There was no sign of Zahara.

"Juliet, do you see her?" I inquired.

"Yes. She went into one of the rooms, but I can't move," she informed me. As soon as the stairwell was clear, I headed to Juliet. I tried not to laugh. Juliet was pinned against the wall appearing to be holding her breath as a small group of young ladies chatted next to her. Her arms were stretched out along the wall and her legs were spread apart. I looked at her and shrugged my shoulders, "I don't know how to help you?" I covered my mouth to try and prevent myself from snickering.

She rolled her eyes at me, "Just go. She entered a room on the left side of the hall a few doors down.

I popped my head through the doors until I found the one with Zahara. It appeared she shared a room with two other girls. The walls of the room were painted in a soft sky blue. They had a small balcony they shared with another dorm. Zahara was the only one in her room at the moment. I pulled out the camera and snapped a picture of her. As soon as I did the camera started making noise as it printed out the picture. Zahara shot a look in my direction. I did not know what to do. I shoved the camera under my shirt to try and muffle the noise, but it did not seem to help. She stood up and started walking in my direction. She had a mirror on her wall by a small refrigerator. I focused on the hallway where Juliet was and teleported there. Juliet seemed to be trying to slither across the wall to get away from the group of teens. She was nearly out from behind them. I grabbed her hand and teleported us both back to my room.

Juliet fell face-first onto my bed and tried to say something into the comforter.

I snorted, "I thought about getting a picture of you sprawled across the wall, but someone might have heard the camera. I..." I started laughing. "I did all I could not to burst out laughing at you right there." My ribs began to hurt from laughing so hard.

Juliet rolled over and began laughing, "You've no idea how scared I was they would lean up against me. I was holding my breath at one point. I think the girl next to me smelled the onions from my omelet I had just before coming here."

Once we calmed down, she asked me if I was able to get a picture of Zahara. This started me going again as I attempted to tell her about the Polaroid camera taking center stage in my mission. We both had a bad case of the giggles. We headed downstairs to get drinks. Phyllis was unloading the dishwasher. In a snooty way, I asked, "Phyllis, do you know the significance of the ten-twenty position?"

"Unless you mean to tell me you are done with your meal, I don't know what you mean," she replied.

Juliet and I burst out laughing. We filled Phyllis in on what had occurred in Switzerland.

"Perhaps you should drop in on that class occasionally. It could be useful," she suggested.

Juliet and I looked at each other. "It certainly wouldn't hurt. I've seen you eat chicken wings, and it's not a pretty sight," Juliet commented with a chuckle.

When it was time for Juliet to head to the University, we rode together. I had some studying I needed to do, and I could always pop home if I need to leave.

Juliet seemed focused on the road. She hardly said a word. I asked, "Are you always this quiet when you drive?"

Juliet glanced over. "Jacob told me the same thing. They always taught me to be quiet in the car to allow the driver to focus. Is there something you want to talk about?"

"Phyllis thinks I need a will to make sure the stone goes to whom I want it to," I informed her.

Without taking her eyes off the road, Juliet replied, "It's a good idea, but who would you give it to. Isn't it supposed to go to a relative of yours?"

"Yes, I had considered Kevin. I don't think he would be up to it after what Eleni did to him. My children were always my first thought. It hadn't occurred to me I might need to find someone until they could take over," I said as I looked in the visor mirror to check my makeup. I thought about how I could ensure the safety of the stone and still someday pass it on to a worthy relative. *Uh, who do I pick?* This question lingered in my mind throughout the day. I texted Phyllis to see if she could make me an appointment with Mr. Thomas.

After class, I texted Juliet to let her know I was heading home. I entered the stall of a nearby restroom. As soon as everyone was gone; I went to my room. I started thinking about Eleni. She was in Greece now. I paid her a visit.

I appeared behind a bush. I walked toward her home and noticed she and a man were sitting on her patio. I walked straight up to her, keeping a six-foot distance. She looked at me and held my gaze for a few seconds. She turned to the man sitting next to her. "This is the kid, that has been giving me so much trouble."

The large, muscular man checked me out. He squinched his face up and said, "This kid?"

I took a step forward and tossed the picture of her daughter at her. Eleni's jaw dropped open. She looked up and asked, "Who gave this to you?"

"It doesn't matter. If you want her to remain a happy fourteen-year-old, you will back off," I warned.

She sat up and looked me dead in the eye. Her face became angry. She asked, "Do you really think you can come in here and threaten me, little one? You will not touch my daughter!"

Her muscle man stood up and said, "You're the one that needs to be worried." He charged at me.

I took off toward the house. Using my parkour skills, I scaled the house and began running across the roof. I looked down at him. He was running along the side of the house. I turned and ran to the other side of the home and pulled out my mirror. I jumped back to Eleni, only invisible this time.

She was on the phone. "Are you sure no one came to see you recently?" There was a pause. She took a picture of the photograph I gave her and sent it to the person on the phone. "They took this picture of you. Who took it?"

I now knew Zahara was on the phone with Eleni.

"Today? How's that possible? It had to be a student or instructor. Are there any Americans there?" Another pause. "Find out. It had to be a student or the faculty." She hung up the phone.

The man returned, out of breath. He struggled to say, "I lost her."

"She didn't just disappear. Keep looking for her," Eleni demanded. "Wait, Zahara needs protection. Have someone assigned to her immediately!"

He ran to the other side of the home. I followed him. He was looking around. He pulled his phone out and called someone. "Start surveillance on Zahara. I need to know where she goes and if she leaves the school. Tell me everyone who visits her. Someone might try to kidnap her." He hung up the phone and continued walking along the side of Eleni's house.

An idea popped into my head. Brooke, you are evil. I giggled and teleported inside the home to Eleni's office. The man searching for me was nearly at the window. Making sure I was visible, I looked out the window and waited for him. As soon as he was within view, I knocked on it. I had his attention.

He looked at me with angry eyes and said, "You're going to get it, kid." He turned and ran.

I chuckled. *He thinks he's going to get me.* I left the room and slipped into the nearby restroom to teleport myself back invisible.

I heard a door slam, followed by the sound of footsteps running in my direction. I peeked through the door and saw him. He was standing in the office's doorway, looking around. He lunged toward the bathroom and flung the door open. I moved my body out of the entrance. He looked in and pulled the door closed. He wandered around the house for a few minutes before heading back to Eleni. I popped over to her.

"She's in the house, but I can't find her," he informed her.

"Must I do everything myself?" She slammed her phone on the table and headed inside.

I considered going in and playing with her, but I could leave a print or something somewhere. I headed back to my bedroom. Eleni seemed like she was still determined to get my necklace. I knew we needed to give her a big scare. The more I thought about how what we do will affect Zahara, the more it bothered me. She was a fourteen-year-old girl being used to scare her mother. I hope we could find another way. The Bloom Keepers need to figure something else out. I started to send a text to them when I received a text from Mechelle.

MECHELLE: Grandma okayed us to use the beach house. Only 6 and no boys in girls' rooms. We need to let her know the dates. I can go whenever.

BROOKE: Great! To confirm it's you, me, Greg, Jacob, and Juliet. Who am I missing?

MECHELLE: I hope Austin.

BROOKE: Austin? Really?? Only teasing you. Greg's waiting for confirmation from you to ask him. I'll get you the dates. Love you.

I texted the Bloom Keepers to let them know we needed to meet. Jacob was the first to respond to the group.

JACOB: I'm working on something. Let's meet when I figure it out. I should have something by Saturday morning.

GREG: How about Cherokee Park at 10 am for the meeting, workout, and lunch?

Everyone agreed to the meeting time.

After dinner, I had some free time on my hands. I dropped in on Kevin and his parents. When I arrived, the three of them were playing dominos at the kitchen table. I startled them when I walked in on them. After a moment of greeting one another. I spent some time hanging out with them, trying to see how Kevin was doing. He seemed to be doing much better. I was hoping Kevin would leave the room to allow me to find out how his parents felt he was doing, but he didn't. He inquired about how things were going with Eleni. I felt it best for their own safety to only disclose we were still working on the situation.

112

Using telepathy, I asked Lainie how she thought he was really doing. She said, "At first, he was having a really hard time, but he's doing much better now. I'm sure he'll feel better when he knows Eleni's no longer a threat."

It comforted me, knowing he was doing better. I asked him if I could speak with him alone. We excused ourselves and went to his bedroom. He sat on the bed, and I sat on the chair in the corner. I explained my reasons for wanting to speak privately, "I need you to be completely honest with me. Are you up to continue as the guardian of the journal?"

"I've had a lot of time to think about it. After what happened, you've every right to wonder if I'm up to the task. At first, I would have said I'm done. I was in shock over what had happened. Something like that could happen again, and I'm pretty sure it will. I was naïve thinking I was untouchable and, frankly, I was not prepared for what they did to me." He shook his head. "Nothing had happened to my parents in years. I'll be prepared the next time. Allison has been training me," he explained.

I smiled and asked, "I'm glad to hear it. I'm considering you as a person to inherit the Bloom of Dreams should anything happen to me. Is that something you would consider?"

"I'm honored, really, but I don't know that I want that much responsibility. It would be one thing for a short time. To take that on for the rest of my life... well, I'm not so sure. I know it should stay in the family, but perhaps one of the Bloom Keepers would take it on until a family member was able to," he said.

I jumped up and kissed him on the cheek, "You're brilliant! When I get all the details worked out, I'll let you know." I said my goodbyes to everyone and headed home.

Sixteen

Juliet told us not to pack a lunch for the park. She and her mother had made a special lunch for us. I expected the day to be beautiful. I was looking forward to all of us working out together, but mostly I wanted to see how Jacob had come along. Greg and I were going to drive over together, and Mom asked him to join us for breakfast. I tried to explain we needed to eat light because we would be working out afterward, but she insisted. To help us out, she had an earlier breakfast. I was near the kitchen when I heard the doorbell chime.XXXmallXXXed it was Greg, but noticed Lance was at the front door.

We greeted one another, and I showed him to the sitting room. I headed to the kitchen to see if my mother was downstairs yet. She wasn't. I called her and she asked me to entertain him until she was ready. *What am I supposed to talk to him about?* "Mom will be down in a few minutes. Can I get you something to drink?" I asked. *Please say yes.*

"No, thanks," he said, fixing the cuff of his shirt.

We were silent for what felt like an eternity. I asked, "Do you and Mom have plans today?"

"Yes. We have a barbeque to attend this afternoon. Your mother told me you and your friends are going to the park today. That should be fun," he said, as he seemed to get more comfortable with me.

I filled him in on some details of our plans. Which started an actual conversation between us. I know I was hard on him, but he seemed to be growing on me. It was not long before my mother joined us. I looked at my watch wondering when Greg would arrive.

A few minutes later, Phyllis announced breakfast. I told her Greg was not here yet.

"Who do you think has been helping me for the last thirty minutes? You can thank Greg for the watermelon balls in the fruit salad," she informed me.

Greg came out with a tray of bowls of fruit salad for everyone. He placed a bowl at each table setting, before giving me a kiss hello. We had a wonderful breakfast. Phyllis was planning on going to her sister's and would be back on Sunday night. Greg and I did the dishes so she could leave. We chatted with Mom and Lance until we had to head to the park.

Jacob and Juliet were stretching when we arrived. "Hey guys," Jacob said as he got off the ground. "Do you mind if we have a meeting first, before the park gets too crowded?"

We sat down at the table next to them and began our meeting. Jacob opened it. I really liked how he took on this role. I felt my emotions becoming overwhelming. Juliet looked over at me. She asked, "Are you okay, Brooke?"

"Yes, I'm sorry Jacob. I'm just so proud of everyone. Watching Jacob lead our meeting got me thinking about all he does for the group. We couldn't have anyone better for our technical electronic thingy. Juliet, you're great at research and can kick some butt. Greg... well, I can't say enough about all you have contributed," I said, bowing my head as a tear fell from my cheek.

Juliet said as she placed her hand on mine, "Ah, Brooke. We can't thank you enough for bringing us into your world."

"I think Brooke would agree. Only God could have brought the four of us together," Greg commented.

"That's it. Group hug," Juliet said as she stood up and made everyone get up for an amazing moment.

After a moment, I pulled away and wiped my eyes. I looked up, and it seemed everyone was a little emotional. "Okay, let's get back to business," I said, settling back into my seat.

Jacob cleared his throat. "Juliet and I were discussing Zahara. We're not completely opposed to the idea of taking her to get her mother to back off, but we might have come up with a better idea."

Grateful to hear those words, I expressed my concerns about our original plan. Jacob continued, "Juliet had the idea to hit her where it hurts. I have access to her accounts and let's just say she doesn't earn all her money legally. We can threaten to expose her money laundering business. This would threaten her lively hood and her reputation if we leaked the information to the press or even the police."

"We could do both. This is a great idea, Juliet," Greg complimented.

"It sounds like we have a new plan. Jacob, get all the evidence you can together. Hopefully, we won't need to use it. I'll talk to Eleni and see if we can persuade her to back off," I said, noticing Greg seemed like he had something to say. "Greg, do you have something to add?"

He chuckled. "I was going to say, I would go with you, but I think we have proven you can handle yourself."

"If it's just her and I'm sure I can handle it, but if I get put in a trap, I'll need backup. You and I will work out the details of the meeting," I explained.

We concluded the meeting and began stretching out. Greg ran to the back of his truck and pulled out the pads we used when sparring. He hollered over to us, "Are we ready to have some fun? Jacob, how about you and Brooke go first?"

I began putting on my pads and said, "I'm not sure this is fair. The only action I've seen him in was in a parking lot." I walked closer to Jacob to get ready for our match. "I've heard you've come a long way. Be nice."

Jacob's cheeks turned pink. He seemed embarrassed by my comment. Each of us bowed to one another. We danced around for a moment. It seemed neither of us wanted to hit the other. *Just go for it.* I swung, and he dodged my attack. "Very good," I commented, just before he blocked my kick. I approached with a punch, which he blocked with his left arm, and with his right fist, he punched my left rib. "Okay... Okay, I see you have developed some skills," I complimented.

Jacob bit his lip and tried not to smile. He charged at me with a few punches, but I was able to block. He was aiming for my head. His height made it strange to fight him. Jacob threw his first kick, which I ducked and swept my leg under his. He fell to the ground. I attempted to get him while he was down, but he recovered and moved back to a standing position.

Greg encouraged Jacob, "Jacob, give her all ya got!"

Looks like I am going to need to be a little more aggressive. I moved forward with a few punches. He could not block all of them. Jacob threw a kick at me, which I was nearly hit. I got myself in the guardian stance. For momentum, I lifted my left leg up, jumped and kicked Jacob in the chest. He fell backward, landing on his back. Jacob had the wind knocked out of him. Immediately, I ran to his side. I placed my hand on his. It appeared he was not being healed. *Why's it not working?* I noticed the stone was dangling from my neck. I grabbed the stone with my left hand. It started working.

Jacob sat up. "Looks like I still have more to learn," he joked. Greg helped him up.

"You've come a long way. You should be proud of yourself," Greg informed him. "Juliet and I have been training together, some with Jacob. Brooke, do you need a break before you spar with Juliet?"

I commented before swallowing a gulp of water, "I'm good." I waited for her to put the pads on.

Greg tossed me a pole and gave Juliet hers when she was ready. We wasted no time. We bowed to one another and immediately started. The poles clanked as we began our battle. Juliet jumped up and came down with the pole. I blocked it from hitting me in the head. She jumped up on the picnic table. I swung the rod at her, but she jumped over it. She flipped over my head and swung the pole behind my legs, knocking me over. A small group was watching us. She reached over and helped me up. We continued our strikes toward one another. At one point, Juliet placed her pole on the ground, holding on to the other end of it, and flipped over me. She dominated me. I was able to strike her a few times, but she knocked me off my feet numerous times. The last time I crashed to the ground, I raised my hands and said, "I'm done."

The small group applauded. I sat down and chugged some water. I looked at Juliet and said, "You're superb."

"I've had years of practice," she said as she wiped the sweat off her forehead.

"It doesn't seem fair Greg has not been able to take part in this workout. Greg needs a challenge," Jacob commented.

Without lifting his head, Greg moved his eyes to Jacob and said, "Okay, who's going to challenge me?"

Jacob smiled, "You misunderstood. I didn't say you needed to be challenged. I said you need a challenge."

Greg scrunched his face. Looking a little concerned he asked, "What do ya mean?"

"Greg, your challenge, should you choose to accept it, is to take all three of us on," Jacob said with a chuckle.

Greg leaned back against the table and crossed his arms. He rubbed his chin with his left hand and looked at each of us one by one. "Okay, but we don't have enough pads for everyone and no poles."

"Jacob can have my pads," I said, handing them to him.

The three of us started by standing next to one another. We bowed to Greg. Jacob asked, "You ready for this?"

"If ya'll are ready," he said, holding his stance. He stuck his left hand, palm up, out and raised his fingers a few times in a motion to tell us to come at him. "Let's go."

I lunged first, which he blocked, and he swung at Juliet. He kicked Jacob, knocking him over. I hit him in the stomach, causing him to bend over. Followed by a knee to his head. Jacob grabbed him from behind, holding his arms down. Juliet threw a punch, hitting him in the head. Greg twisted and kicked her, which pushed her away. He twisted out of Jacob's arms and flung him to the ground with a few punches to his abdomen. The battle continued for a few minutes. Each of us was able to get a few strikes in. Greg defended himself well. He was knocked closer to the small crowd that was watching us but recovered quickly.

Our sparring ended when the police showed up. We immediately became motionless. The officer came over and asked us what was going on. "We were just sparring, officer," Greg informed him.

The officer told the crowd to move along. He turned to Greg and said, "Sparring, huh? Someone called in saying a young man was beating up a few people."

"Greg, I guess that means you won that match," Jacob commented.

We all chuckled. The officer told us to make sure everyone had protection if we did this again. He asked us not to spar anymore today. He stayed and talked to us for a few minutes before leaving. We went for a short hike until returning to Juliet's vehicle for lunch.

Jacob brought the cooler to the picnic table. Juliet announced, "We have a blueberry and watermelon salad with basil. I also brought Hawaiian chicken salad with apples and pineapple. Oh, there's bottled water too."

Lunch was delicious. There was nothing left for her to take home. We began discussing the summer break to work out dates.

Juliet asked everyone to provide her dates we were not available, and she would work out a few different weeks for Mechelle's grandmother to pick from. We did not want to demand a specific time frame.

Juliet asked, "Would you mind healing me? I don't want to explain all the bruises I'm going to have." I reached over and grabbed her hand. The stone heated up. I felt Jacob and Greg place their hands on me to be healed, as well. Once everyone healed. We packed up everything and headed home to clean up.

Saturday night, I had dinner with Greg's family, and we played Monopoly with them. It was wonderful seeing his mother with more energy. Greg had sat me next to her. I think he was hoping I would reach over and heal her, but it was too soon still. We needed to wait a bit to let her scars heal.

I was determined to spend my time after church studying. Finals were coming up. I wanted to make sure I was prepared. Especially if Eleni showed up, and I suddenly had a change in my schedule. I allotted enough time to read over and make some final changes to some letters I had written for the attorney. I wrote a letter to each of the Bloom Keepers to be given if I passed away. They needed to be perfect. Once finished, I crashed for the night.

Seventeen

After cleaning up after my workout, I went to the library to study some more before class. I ran into James. He asked, "Did you see our grade on the presentation?"

It had escaped my mind, "No, I haven't had time to look. How did we do?"

"We got a 98%. We make a great team. Thanks for being my partner," he said before heading off.

I continued studying until my class began. I was so focused in the library, but in my class, I found it difficult to concentrate. My mind focused on my meeting this afternoon with Mr. Thomas. I prayed about what should happen to the Bloom of Dreams, should something happen to me. I prayed I would make the right decision. This was a lot of responsibility to put on someone. Especially someone my age. I'm about to put the same responsibility on someone else.

After class, I raced to Mr. Thomas's office for my appointment. I was a few minutes late, but they immediately escorted me into his office. He had a large corner office with expensive fishing paraphernalia decorating his walls and shelves. On the wall was a picture of him with a young boy, both holding large bass. The receptionist asked me to have a seat and told me he would be with me soon. Looking at the picture of Mr. Thomas brought back memories of my last meeting with him. It was the day that changed my life. My grandmother gave me her most prized possession to protect. *Miss you Grandma.* I continued thinking about her until Mr. Thomas raced in and apologized for being late. He held out his hand for me to shake. *Do I stand? I don't know. He's waiting…* I reached out and shook his hand. *Note to self: take etiquette classes.*

Mr. Thomas sat down and said, "So, Ms. Garrison, you want a will. Is that correct?"

"Yes, Phyllis recommended I have one. With the funds, I'm to inherit and those I received from my grandmother. I should have a will," I informed him.

Mr. Thomas looked over his spectacles at me. "Brooke, you seem wiser than your age," He commented before asking me a bunch of questions about my assets, personal data, and things. "Those were the straightforward questions. Now, who do you want to receive and what are they to get?"

"I've thought about this a lot. I want my funds to go into a trust. The trustee will be Mechelle. She spells her name with all e's no i's. I have a letter I would like her to receive at the reading of the will. I placed it on his desk. This necklace and the compact mirror I received from my grandmother will be given to my cousin Kevin Davis, along with this letter. I placed it on top of the other letter. Greg Scrogham, Juliet Kai, and Jacob Dillard will receive a letter from me as well." I placed their letters with the others. "This is very important. Everyone that receives a letter must burn it when they're done reading them," I explained.

"It would seem you and Lillie think alike," Mr. Thomas said as he took his glasses off and placed them on the desk. "These letters will remain sealed until you collect them, or they are given to the recipient upon your death. I must tell you in all my career, you and Lillie are the only ones that have ever asked to have letters burned after they're read."

"Perhaps we prefer to say our peace and not have the person dwell on our words afterward," I provided him with something to ponder.

"When you put it that way, it makes sense. I must admit, I thought perhaps you had some family secret that needed to be passed down. I guess I let my imagination wander a bit much. Okay, now these letters will be put in our company's safe. I'll have a draft of the will available to you in a week. Once you approve the draft, we'll have you sign the original. I'll provide you with as many copies as you need. Do you have any questions?"

"No," I responded.

He sat back in his chair and said, "As the trustee of your trust, I can allow my payment to come from the trust, or would you rather pay from your personal account?"

"I didn't know that was an option. Please take it from the trust. Thanks." I shook his hand and left his office. As I pushed the entrance door to his building open, I had a sense of pride. I felt like an adult. None of my friends had wills. Most of them owned so little it did not matter. I felt a skip in my step as I walked to my car. In my head, I was playing a tune.

I was not paying attention to anything at that moment including the stone. Suddenly, I felt someone place something over my mouth. I fell to the ground. Using telepathy, I called out to Mr. Thomas, but heard nothing. I was so tired. I noticed I was lying on the ground on my side. The Bloom's not touching me...

Am I in a cocoon? I can't move. So groggy. Drugged? I tried to open my eyes. Everything was blurry. *What's going on?* I felt myself dozing off and waking several more times. I was confused.

The drug was wearing off. I could finally see. There was a small light on. I was back in the basement. I looked down and notice duct tape wrapped around me several times. They tied my hands behind my back. It felt like my wrists were bound with zip ties. I looked down at the duct tape and noticed the Bloom of Dreams was gone. At first, I wanted to cry. *What would my grandmother do? Duh, she would escape.*

My feet were not tied. I waddled myself over to the wall. I got my feet positioned to get myself to a standing position. With my upper body covered in duct tape, I could not get my arms in front of me. *Okay, Brooke, find something to get this tape off.* Just to the right of the stairs was a metal shelf. The shelf contained old paint and spray cans of different chemicals. *Well, there's not much here.* I scanned the room and when I came back to the shelf; I noticed the corners of the shelf were square. Using my foot, I scooted the shelf away from the wall. I placed the front corner of the shelf between my legs. I positioned myself to have that corner at an angle. With enough friction, I could eventually tear through the duct tape. I started moving up and down. All I managed to do was push the shelving back to the wall.

I repositioned the shelf, making sure the other side was against the wall. I repeated the process. It was working. The shelving was staying in place. I repeated this process until I was so exhausted that I had to stop. I looked down. The process was working, but it was moving at a snail's pace. I walked around to see if I could find anything else. There was nothing else to use.

I repeated the process over and over. My legs were burning from so many squats. I had been doing this for what I imagine was hours. I laid down and rested for a while. When I woke, the room immediately reminded me of my situation. I returned to the shelving. My legs were sore. I looked, and I made it through another layer of tape. This motivated me. It did not appear there was much more, but again I grew tired. I leaned up against the wall. I remembered I hid a bottle of water and a granola bar in the box in the corner. There was no way to open either of them at this point.

This motivated me to continue working. The pain in my legs was affecting my focus. I took a deep breath in and closed my eyes. "Lord, I need your help. Please give me the strength to continue," I prayed. My prayer led me to think about how long I had been there. I did not know. *Does anyone know I'm missing?* I needed to stop bringing myself down and focus on my mission.

It felt like the shelving was mocking me. I glared at the shelving. "You'll not defeat me," I snarled at it. This time, I was pushing my shoulder into the corner of the shelving as hard as I could. I concentrated on my breathing to take my mind off the pain. So focused on the motion my body was doing, I did not notice the tape break until I felt the metal scraping my arm. I shed happy tears before realizing I was not out of the woods yet.

I went over to the banister and rubbed the tape along it to break my arm free. It took some time, but I released my right arm. I sat down on the ground and worked to move my hand under my butt. *The Bloom Keepers need to do this workout.* I had a heck of a time getting my hand over my feet. When I finally did, I fell backward and took a brief rest. With my left leg bent back, I slowly worked on untying my shoestring. I could not move my left arm enough. I started trying to pull my body shirt off. It wasn't easy, but I finally got it. It took some work, but I got both shoes untied. I wrapped the string around the zip tie and tied it to my other shoestring. *Now the work begins.* I laid on my back and began moving my feet back and forth, creating friction to burn through the zip ties. I was finally free. *Thank you, Jesus!* I never would have guessed I would have a use for this. *Thank you to whoever posted the video on how to do this.*

I ran over and grabbed the water and the granola bar. I devoured the granola bar and sipped the water. The room was probably locked. I needed to figure out how to get out of the basement. I pulled and pushed on the door. It did not budge. The hinges! They were on the other side of the door. I sat on the stairs, thinking about how I could get through the door. It was the only exit. There were no windows. Defeated was the best way to describe how I felt. I was exhausted and hungry. I took a nap in hopes I could think clearly if I rested.

A loud bang woke me. I looked up and saw a figure running toward me. My eyes focused. It was Greg. He grabbed me and held me tightly. We need to go. Greg helped me up. I followed him up the stairs. We turned toward the front door. Spiro was on the ground, tied up with duct tape. I stopped.

"Come on, Brooke. We need to get out of here," Greg said, pulling my arm and led me to his truck.

Neither of us said anything until we were on the main road. "I knew something was wrong when you did not respond to my texts or calls. Everyone has been so worried about you," Greg informed me.

They had every right to worry. I asked, "How long was I gone?"

"Two days. Jacob discovered Eleni had arrived today. She's staying in her same suite," Greg started explaining.

"Mom must be so worried," I said, staring out the window.

Greg said, "Juliet and Phyllis have been covering for you. Your mom thinks you have been over at Juliet's house."

I interrupted, "Pull into McDonald's." Greg got me a combo meal and a couple of waters. I began chowing down on them. While he waited for a break in the traffic to pull out, he watched me devour the food.

"Eleni's planning on leaving in the morning to head back to Greece. Jacob said her flight's at 10:00 am. Brooke, she has the Bloom of Dreams," he said.

It was making sense. Spiro drugged me and took the necklace. He must have called her, and she came over to get it.

Greg continued, "We need to get to her room and get the stone back. Jacob has full access to deplete her accounts." We pulled up to a light, and he looked over at me. "I know you have been through a lot, but you can rest once we have the necklace."

With a full stomach, I closed my eyes and drifted off to sleep. Greg awoke me. I looked around and asked, "Where are we?"

"We are a few blocks from Eleni's hotel. I didn't want to have anyone know what vehicle we were in," Greg explained.

"Clean yourself up a bit. You're looking a little rough," Greg advised. He reached in the back seat and pulled out a clean t-shirt and handed it to me. "Your shirt's torn and filthy. Put that on. It will draw less attention to you." He reached into the compartment in his armrest and pulled out a brush.

I took it. My hair was full of knots. The brush got caught in my hair. It was a nightmare to get through. Greg handed me a hair tie and said, "Here. Karen always leaves one or two in here." I put my hair up in a ponytail.

"Now for the last part of your new outfit," he said, handing me a ball cap. "Keep your head down and try not to look at any cameras as we move through the hotel." He reached back and grabbed another ball cap and put it on.

I got out of his truck and noticed he had a plastic bag with some items in it. "What's in the bag?"

"Gloves for us. Now keep your head down," he instructed.

I followed him to the hotel. We walked in acting as if we knew where we were going. We got on the elevator. Greg pushed the button with the bag between his finger and the button to ensure we did not leave fingerprints.

"When we get to the door, take your hat off and disguise your voice. Make sure you're not facing the door. We need her to think you're housekeeping," Greg instructed.

We reached her door. Greg handed me a pair of gloves and put a pair on himself. I took a deep breath. Greg grabbed my hat and knocked on the door. I turned so she would only see my ponytail. I heard something on the other side of the door. *She must be looking out.*

Eleni asked, "Who is it?"

"It's management," I said in my best British accent.

Greg shot me a look. The door unlocked and as she opened it; we pushed our way in. Suddenly, I was awake and ready to take back my property. Greg shut the door and put my cap back on.

"Well, you're clever, Brooke", she said, turning and walking farther into her suite.

"Something told me you would never open the door for housekeeping, but I was sure you would want to hear what management would do to make your stay more comfortable," I commented as I followed her. "You took something from me, and I want it back."

She opened her blouse, revealing the Bloom of Dreams. "Now, this belongs to the Greeks. I'm curious, though, how are you going to hurt me when it can heal me immediately?"

126

I reached down and felt my pocket. They never took the mirror. She must not know of all its powers.

Greg pulled out his phone and called someone. *Does he really think this is a time for a personal call?* We both looked at him. "Eleni, you will give it back to me if I have to rip it off your neck," I said sternly, taking a stance to begin a battle.

"Eleni, we don't have to touch you to cause you pain. Perhaps you should look at that special account you have. You know, the one with all of your laundered money," Greg instructed her as he moved a little closer to me.

Eleni was sweating. She moved toward the coffee table and picked up her phone. She began searching and suddenly stopped, "Oh please, you're just kids. What could you possibly do?"

Greg spoke into his phone, "Send her the files."

Eleni's phone dinged. She lifted it and began reading. Greg leaned over to me and said, "She was just sent the evidence we have on her."

Thank God for Jacob! I moved a little closer.

Her face appeared to be frozen as she read, "How... Where did you get this?"

"Eleni, there's more. See, we were thinking it would be great to take the funds you have gained illegally and make a sizeable donation to some orphanages or something. We would send it in your name, of course. We would make sure the press knew about your generous side. That way, you could not take the funds back because it would destroy your reputation," Greg explained the rest of the plan.

She scrunched up her face and flung forward, "You wouldn't!"

"You know we would. He just needs to say the word," I added.

"If you want it, you'll have to take it from me. You should know I'm not going to give it to you willingly," she snapped.

"It'll be my pleasure," I turned to Greg, "I got this." I moved toward her. She lunged at me, reaching for my throat. I dodged her. Eleni turned and came back. I threw a kick backward toward her. I flung her body against the wall. She looked at Greg, who seemed to be giving Jacob a play-by-play.

I threw a punch in her abdomen. She hunched over. I jumped up and swung my right leg over her shoulder, and grabbed my ankle with my left hand. My left leg moved and wrapped around the ankle. I wrapped my arms around her head and brought her to the ground. She could not move.

She blurted out, "I can't breathe."

Greg removed the necklace from her neck. I released her. She collapsed to the floor, trying to catch her breath. I asked, "Wouldn't it have been easier to just give it to me?"

Greg placed the necklace around my neck and latched it. Immediately, I felt it healing me.

Eleni giggled.

Greg asked, "What's so funny?"

"I didn't give you the necklace. It's not going to work," she chuckled again. She seemed in pain as she tried to pull herself up.

I took one rubber glove off and pushed her over the back of the sofa. I grabbed her arm and pulled it behind her back to hold her in that position. She tried to get away, but I held her tightly while the stone healed her. I released my grip.

Eleni stood up. She looked confused. Sarcastically she asked, "How's it working?"

"You shouldn't mess with things you know nothing about. Now, I suggest you forget about this stone. If you even glance in my direction after I leave here, your actions will dramatically impact your life. Everything we have on you will be given to the authorities and we'll deplete every account you have," I said, as I picked up the ball cap I dropped during the fight. Just before leaving, I turned back to her, "Get out of my town."

We made our way to the stairs out of fear there might be a camera in the elevator and teleported back to his truck. Greg started heading home. I was exhausted and in need of a shower. "Do you mind if I just go home.? I don't want anyone seeing me like this," I asked.

Greg understood, "Ya know I love ya, but you're smelling a little rank, too."

I showered and crashed into my bed for a few hours.

Eighteen

I woke up and reached for my phone. It was gone. I needed to find it. Perhaps it was in the basement. I popped over and began searching. It was not there. I began searching the first floor. Spiro was still lying there. I lightly kicked him to get him to wake up. "Where's my phone?" He tried to speak, but the tape was hindering him. "If you tell me where my phone is, I'll release you?" I ripped the tape off his mouth.

"In the trash," he said. I headed for the kitchen. "Hey wait! You promised to untie me," he hollered.

I grabbed the trash can and dumped it on the counter. The last thing I wanted was to dig through the waist. I took a wooden spoon from the utensil carousel and began pushing the trash around. My phone was underneath a coffee filter. I grabbed a towel from the counter and wiped it off. The phone was dead. I walked back into the living room and removed the duct tape from Spiro's hands, but left his feet tied. "Contact Eleni. I'm sure you can return to Greece," I said, walking back into the kitchen. I pulled out my mirror and returned home to plug my phone in.

Once my phone came back on, I read the many texts I received. It was apparent with the number of texts, the Bloom Keepers were concerned about me. I had not noticed the time. Class was in ten minutes. I got dressed and teleported to the bathroom down the hall from my classroom. I was only a few minutes late. The professor was reviewing the final exam information. I tried to stay focused on what he was saying, but I had a hard time.

The class ended. Out of habit, I walked to the parking lot. With all that was going on I had forgotten I did not drive to school. The sun was shining on my face. I closed my eyes and took in the warmth.

"Brooke!"

Did someone call me? I opened my eyes and looked around. I saw Juliet running toward me.

"Brooke, wait for me," she hollered.

She about knocked me down with her hug. "Greg told me where he found you. I'm so glad you're okay," she said, holding me tightly.

"I'm fine," I said, pulling myself away. "Really, we need to meet. Do you think everyone could meet today?"

Juliet pulled out her phone and began texting Greg and Jacob. "Let's head to the library and see about getting a room." We made our way there and were able to secure the room. Juliet had only heard from Jacob. "He should be here shortly."

She and I waited in the room. Juliet was staring at me, "What is it, Juliet?"

"I'm sorry, I keep thinking about how we couldn't help you," she said with tears in her eyes.

"Juliet, I'm not going to say it's easy. There was not a doubt in my mind you guys would figure out I was gone and praying got me through it. Besides, I slept a lot," I said, to lighten the mood.

Jacob flung the door open. His eyes teared up, "It's good to have you back," He smiled. "Has anyone heard from Greg?"

Juliet shook her head. I haven't heard from him.

I called him, "There's a meeting. Where are you?"

"When ya left the truck, I wanted to make sure Eleni was on her way back to Greece. I went back to her hotel. Spiro showed up. They're on the plane now. I needed to know she took our threat seriously. I'm sorry I did not answer. I needed to know she was no longer a danger to ya," Greg paused. "I love ya and I didn't protect ya. I'm so sorry," he said, sounding as if he was fighting tears.

"I'll be right back," I said, pulling out my mirror. "Greg, pull over," I instructed. I looked out the window into the library and saw no one there and vanished from the room.

I appeared in Greg's truck. He was pulling the truck to the hazard lane. He turned to me with his arms open, "I'm so sorry." He began to sob.

We embraced for a moment. The comfort of his arms seemed to heal all that had happened. I kissed him. He kissed me back with passion. Our bodies were like magnets, clinging to one another. Part of me never wanted to leave the comfort of his embrace. I kissed him again and pulled myself away.

"This is not your fault. It was mine. I was not paying attention to my surroundings and was caught unexpectedly. I used the skills you had taught me to free myself. Well, you and YouTube. I had about given up when I couldn't get the basement door open," I said, wiping a tear from my cheek. "You showed up and set me free."

Greg wiped the tears from his eyes, "You head back to the meeting. I'm not up to it. Call me when you get home." He placed his hand on my cheek and ran his thumb across it before giving me another kiss.

I returned to the library, "Greg's not going to be here. I'll fill him in later." I sat down. I started the story with how Spiro captured me. I concluded with us leaving Eleni.

Juliet filled me in on what I missed, "Greg thought it was strange he had not heard from you. We all started trying to reach you. Jacob checked to see if Eleni was in town. She had just arrived a few hours before his search. He discovered Spiro was still here. That led Greg to look at that house we went to. Jacob discovered she was planning to leave the next day, which is why Greg took you to her hotel. I believe you're up to date."

"Greg did text us to tell us you were okay. Oh, and you had the necklace back," Jacob added.

I commented, "I need to talk to all the Bloom Keepers. Tomorrow afternoon, can you be at my house by 3:30?"

They said they could. "Dress nicely," I said as I picked up my backpack and pulled out my mirror. I checked to make sure no one could see me and headed to Kevin and his family. Lainie and Kevin were in the kitchen. William was reading a book at the table. "I have some news," I announced. "Eleni will no longer be bothering us. Pack your things and I will bring you home the day after tomorrow."

I quickly explained what we threatened her with and told them to be ready tomorrow at 3:15 pm and to dress appropriately.

I left and headed to Mechelle's dorm. She was napping. I tickled her to wake her up. It surprised her to see me. After a quick recap of the meeting, she assured me she would be ready.

I did not know where Allison would be, so I used the special phone she gave me to invite her. "Thank you for the invite, but I must decline. With my job, it's better no one knows I'm involved with the stone's protection," Allison explained. To change her mind, I told her the reason for the meeting.

"I really must decline. If the stone ever switches hands, I will contact the person who replaces you. I'm sure you will be responsible for it for many more years," she informed me.

I filled her in on the plans for the stone, should something happen to me. We spent a few minutes catching up before I was off to Italy. I dropped my backpack on the bed and headed down to find Isabella and Leonardo. They were enjoying dinner with one of their guests. I asked the server to have them come to join me.

Isabella asked, "Is everything okay?"

I answered, "Yes. I'm sorry for interrupting your dinner, but I have a favor to ask. Is there somewhere more private we can talk?"

Leonardo led us through the kitchen to a walk-in refrigerator. "We should not be disturbed here."

"Tomorrow, around 9:15 pm, I would like to have a small party for a special announcement for the Bloom Keepers. Nothing extravagant. Just some appetizers and drinks. Perhaps we could use the wine cellar," I suggested.

Isabella assured me, "That can easily be done. How many of us will there be?"

"There should be eleven, which includes both of you," I answered.

I gave them a hug and headed back. When I got home, I texted Greg to let him know I was home, but he did not respond to me. I ran down to see Phyllis. She was placing food into a basket. I asked, "What are you up to? Do you have a hot date or something?"

Phyllis turned around and hugged me tightly. "Child, you put a scare on me." She pulled away and started forcing me to turn around. "Turn around. I need to know my baby's not hurt."

I span around. "Your baby's fine." I ended my spin with jazz hands.

"Greg told me what happened. He was beside himself with worry. That boy loves you," Phyllis said as Greg opened the back door with a single red rose in his hand. He kissed Phyllis on the cheek and gave her the rose. It was so sweet.

Greg turned to me and pulled an enormous bouquet he had hidden behind his back for me. I kissed him and thanked him for the beautiful flowers. I put them in a delicate vase.

"I'm busy here. Why don't you kids go hang out in the sitting room for a few more minutes?" Phyllis sounded as if she was ordering us to go.

Greg grabbed my hand and pulled me toward the doorway. I pulled back and popped a piece of carrot from the salad into my mouth. Then grabbed the flowers before following him. I placed the flowers on the table in the foyer. We went into the sitting room. Greg and I sat on the sofa snuggling. I explained to him about the meeting the next day and to dress nicely. He tried to get information from me. He even attempted to get it from me using tickle torture, but like the others, he was going to need to wait.

Phyllis hollered for Greg. He told me he would be right back. He was gone for a few minutes. Phyllis came in and told me Greg was out back waiting for me. *What's that boy up to?* I walked out the back door and found Greg standing by the patio table. He covered the plants in twinkle lights, and the fire pit had a small fire going. Greg set the table for two.

"Please have a seat," Greg said, pulling a chair out for me. Behind him was a cooler. He reached in and pulled out a thermos. Greg poured the soup into each of our bowls and sat down next to me. He said grace, and we began enjoying the chicken soup. Once we finished, he removed the bowls and reached into the cooler, and pulled out a couple of plastic containers. He placed a piece of chicken with what smelled like white wine and rosemary sauce. The second one contained rice pilaf and the third one was green beans.

He sat down and suddenly jumped up and lit the candles on the table. "Sorry, I forgot," he muttered.

"Greg, this is so sweet. I really appreciate all the effort you went through to set this up," I said as I cut my chicken.

"Phyllis cooked everything. I helped her pack it up, and I told her I would do all the dishes," he explained.

We continued eating and discussing what we would like to do during our summer trip to Myrtle Beach. The meal was wonderful. He cleared the table and said he would be back in a few minutes. He carried a few of the dishes into the kitchen and returned with a tray. He placed the tray on the table by the fire pit.

Greg came over and held his hand out and said, "Please join me by the fire."

I sat down on the bench. He handed me a metal skewer and handed me a bowl of marshmallows. As our marshmallows roasted,

Greg opened up to me, "Brooke, what happened to you, scared me. I thought I lost you and I felt like I failed you. Before this, I knew I loved you. I just didn't know how much. Honestly, I never knew anyone could love someone more than their own life. You are the best thing to happen to me. I can't picture my life without you. Heck, one day I want us to have lots of kids," he said.

I didn't know what to say. I felt the same way. Shocked was the best way to describe how I felt. Greg was so open about his feelings. I leaned over and kissed him gently. I let my lips linger on his. We snuggled up next to one another. Periodically exchanging kisses. The evening was perfect. Phyllis did some of the dishes while we were out. Greg and I finished the rest of them. Greg and I spent a few minutes making out before we said goodnight to one another. Just as he started to walk home, I said, "I want to have lots of babies with you too." He turned around and smiled.

I walked back inside, and Mom was behind me. "I'm sorry for being so late. How was your day?" We chatted about my evening before we both headed to bed.

Nineteen

I was so excited about the evening; I picked out the cutest dress. The dress was predominately blue. It tied around my neck. It had sleeves but left my shoulders bare. I wanted to look beautiful for Greg. Fortunately, I did not have a class this afternoon. I curled my hair and took my time to make sure my makeup looked perfect. I looked at myself in the mirror and spun around to see how my dress flowed. It was perfect.

Phyllis had me take her to the villa early. She wanted to help Isabella with setting everything up. I headed to Mechelle. She was excited about seeing everyone again. After dropping her off in the wine cellar, I brought Kevin and his parents. I returned to the house. Juliet and Jacob were waiting at the front door when I arrived. They both looked so nice. Juliet noticed my flowers. I told her what Greg had done for me.

Greg showed up a few minutes after them. He was wearing a navy-blue shirt, a blue blazer, and cream slacks. I had never seen him look so nice. I gave him a hug. He was wearing the cologne I love so much. His love potion was working again. We moved away from the window, and I took us to the wine cellar. The room looked beautiful. There were wine barrels being used as cocktail tables and several barrels were lined up with a nice board on top of them making a stunning table setting for the food. The food was placed on different levels. There was a variety of meat, cheese, and fruit to eat. Greg went over to say hello to everyone. I stayed back and took in the evening. Everyone was chatting and having a good time.

My love for the people in this room filled me with joy. I had gained an extended family. The people in this room knew my deepest secrets. I took my glass and clanked my fork on it to get everyone's attention. Everyone turned and waited for me.

"I have asked you here today because everyone here is part of the Bloom Keepers. We are an important team created to protect the safety of the Bloom of Dreams and those chosen to help with its protection. You're more than that to me, your family. The protection of the stone concerns everyone in this room. It was brought to my attention I needed a will to ensure the Bloom of Dreams remains safe after I'm gone. Traditionally the stone is passed down to a family member. Being a part of this group and being at one with the stone are very different responsibilities and require different skills. Currently, I don't have a candidate to replace me, but I have come up with a way to ensure it's always protected. A few of you do not know Mechelle." I motioned for her to join me.

Mechelle and I have been friends most of our lives. She, like a few of you, accidentally found out about my new powers. She will generally have little to do with the day-to-day of the Bloom Keepers, but I trust her with my life. My current trust will move from Mr. Thomas as trustee to Mechelle. Leonardo and Isabella, we need to make the same arrangement for the trust you hold should something happen to either of you or if you choose to step down.

A few faces seemed surprised by the news of a second trust. Even Mechelle seemed surprised by my announcement. She leaned over to me and whispered, "Are you sure?"

"Very," I said assuring her. I turned back to the group and continued, "My cousin Kevin and his family have been protecting the secret of the Book of Dreams for decades. Kevin Davis will be inheriting the Bloom of Dreams and my grandmother's compact mirror. Kevin, you will determine who in the family's ability to handle the responsibility of the Bloom of Dreams at the time of my death if I have not already appointed someone. If no one in the family's worthy, you are to choose either Greg Scrogham, Juliet Kai, or Jacob Dillard. They'll be responsible for it until a relative can be chosen. Now, everyone enjoy yourselves."

Mechelle came over, "I'm shocked. Thank you. That's a lot of responsibility."

"I know you can handle it. You understand the job, you're great with money. I know you'll do what's best for the Bloom's safety," I assured her.

Leonardo walked up to us. He said, "Mechelle, it sounds like we need to talk. Would you mind following me to my office? I need to get some information from you." They headed out of the cellar.

Lainie and William approached me. "Your choices were brilliant to ensure your legacy remains safe. Lillie would be very proud of you."

I thanked them. Kevin and Greg joined us. "I'll make sure someone in the family's prepared to take over the responsibility. I think the group you chose to work directly with should help me develop the person as well as choose them," Kevin said.

"That would be an honor. Thanks," Greg told him.

Isabella came over. "How about some music?"

I nodded.

"I guess I need a dance partner," Kevin strolled over to the punch table and started talking to Isabella.

Greg wrapped his arms around me. "I'm proud of ya. It must've been difficult to make these decisions. Ya made the right ones." He leaned down and kissed me. "Now let's show them how to do this." Greg led me to the dance floor. For a while, we danced. We were enjoying a slow dance when Phyllis tapped me on the shoulder. "We need to get back. Your mother will be home shortly," she advised.

She was right. I had Isabella turn off the music. *We need to do this again soon.* I explained we needed to leave. I took Mechelle home first. I told Greg that I would bring him back with me once I had everyone else back. He had everyone help clean up while I took Kevin and his parents back. We returned to their safe house. They needed to pack. I promised to come back the next day to take them home. Before leaving, I told Kevin to let me know when he wanted to move the journal to a safe location. He explained he needed to find one first.

I made two trips, bringing everyone back home. Phyllis was about to change to prepare dinner. I suggested we all go out to eat because I did not want the evening to end. Greg went home. Phyllis and I waited for Mom before heading out.

Everyone had a great time. It filled my heart with joy. Today had been perfect. The evening was nearly over. Greg and I said our good nights on the front porch. "You looked amazing tonight," Greg said.

I thanked him and wrapped my arms around him. I tilted my head to look him in the eyes. My heart was fluttering. We began kissing. My body tingled. Our desire for one another was unmistakable, but we both knew when to stop before we took it farther than we should. We told each other I love you before heading into our homes.

It had been a long day but was still early. I spent the rest of the evening studying before heading to bed.

The next day, I buckled down hard, studying for my finals. The class went well. I felt like I was back on track with my schoolwork. I set up a couple of study sessions with other students to ensure it would prepare me for my other exams. My schedule for the next week was going to be busy. After class, I headed home to drop my things off before taking Kevin and his family back to their condominium.

When I arrived, they had luggage stacked by the front door and were sitting in the living room waiting for me. "I guess you're all ready to go," I said as I entered the room. They all stood up. "I'm excited about getting back to my normal routine. My friends must be worried about me," Lainie announced.

I had forgotten they could not use their phones or to have contact with anyone. "What will your cover story be?"

"We are going to tell everyone we headed for a retreat in the mountains and there was no cell service," William explained.

William and Kevin each grabbed a few suitcases. I did as well. Lainie had a small bag and her purse. I took them to Kevin's home. It was still a mess. Kevin looked around in shock. I asked, "Do you want some help to clean up?"

"No, I'll take care of it. Let's go get the rest of the bags," he said as he grabbed my arm. We brought back the rest of the bags. Kevin's parents were already gone when we returned. "I figured out where to hide the journal," I left to retrieve it for him.

I returned and made another entry into the journal before giving it back to Kevin. He hugged me and said, "Thank you for saving me."

I squeezed him tightly and said, "I'm glad you are doing better. Keep in touch." I headed home for another night of studying.

I could not meet with Mr. Thomas the following week. My class schedule and study groups did not leave me a lot of time slots. The few I had available, he had appointments. I made an appointment for the following week after my finals.

Working around my classmate's schedules, we decided to meet at 9:30 am. I got up early for my workout. Greg reluctantly joined me at

7:00 am. It was a beautiful morning. We started with a three-mile run and ended with more training and a few minutes of sparring.

"I should get ya and Austin together for some sparring. He's a bit out of practice. I think ya could whip him back into shape." Greg laughed.

"Sounds fun." I responded. I kissed him and headed home for a shower.

Twenty

The study groups went well. I took a break for the weekend. I felt prepared for my exams. Jacob's parents invited us over for Jacob's birthday. It was a picnic lunch at his home. I wrapped the gift; Greg and I got him before getting dressed. Greg picked me up right on time. On the drive over, we talked about how excited we were for a summer break. Juliet sent Mechelle the dates, and we were waiting to hear from her on the date. It was great they were becoming friends. Mechelle told me she and Austin were talking, too.

The further we drove, the more the smell of sweat filled the air. I turned to Greg and asked, "What's that stench?"

He glanced in my direction. "What are you talking about?"

I cracked my window to get the foul stench to leave. "It smells… It smells like a locker room." I turned to look in the back seat and found the sparring gear. "Well, I found the source of the odor. These need to be washed," I said, picking up the headgear.

We pulled up to Jacob's house. Juliet had already arrived. Greg grabbed the present. We walked up to the front door, holding hands. Jacob answered, "Hey, come on in. Thanks for coming." He walked us into the dining room where Juliet was helping Jacob's mother. "Ma, this is Greg and Brooke," Jacob introduced us.

"It's so nice to meet you finally. Call me Jane," she said. "Go introduce them to your father."

Juliet took the present and placed it with a few others on the kitchen table. Jacob took us to the living room. His father was watching a documentary about unsolved mysteries. He introduced us to Marty, who asked us to have a seat.

Marty turned the television off. "I've heard a lot about the two of you. You seemed to be a wonderful influence on my boy," he said proudly.

"He's been a wonderful influence on us as well. Your son's very talented," I said. Regrettably, he will never know how his son is a hacker and could easily work for the CIA or FBI.

"Smart too," Greg added.

"As a child, he would sit on my lap and watch me work. Computers have always fascinated him. I'm sure he knows more than he lets on to me. I work for IBM downtown and Jacob has been interning there for the past two summers. He'll be there again this summer," Marty explained.

"Really? That's cool," Greg said to Jacob.

"Thanks," he said.

I asked, "Will that affect your being able to join us in Myrtle Beach?"

"No, I just need to give the dates as soon as possible. I fill in for people when I intern. They need to make sure they have the staff's vacations covered," Jacob said.

Jane came in and asked everyone to help carry everything outside. Marty started up the grill. Everyone sat down at the table with Jane.

"Jacob's closed mouth about most things. We've learned a little about you from Juliet. She speaks highly of you both," Jane said.

"The four of us have become very close friends. I predict we'll be friends forever," I said with a smile. We continued getting to know one another while Marty cooked the burgers.

Once lunch was served, Marty said grace for us. "This is Jacob's favorite lunch," Jane informed us.

"I haven't found many things Jacob doesn't love to eat," Juliet commented.

Lunch was delicious. Jane brought the cake out. We sang to Jacob. Jane asked Greg to help her inside. The three of us talked about exams while Marty cleaned the grill. They returned with Jacob's presents. Jacob seemed embarrassed opening them in front of us. He opened the ones from his parents first. He received clothes and a gas card. Juliet gave him a card explaining to him she was taking him to the mega caverns on Sunday. He finally opened our gift.

"Wow! Thanks," he said excitedly.

Jane asked, "What is it?"

Jacob lifted the headgear and gloves. "Greg and Brooke gave me sparring gear. Thanks guys," he said with a smile.

Jane seemed surprised. She asked, "How much is he really learning? Do you think he'll be using this much?"

Greg stood up. "Jacob, let's show them what you've learned. I got my gear in the car." Greg headed to his truck.

"I think you'll be surprised at what you're about to witness," Juliet said with a chuckle.

I said, "We have three sets of pads. Who wants to spar?"

"Greg takes on the three of us. Perhaps it should be me against the two of you," Jacob said.

Greg returned with the gear. We told him who was going first. We dressed.

"This smells," Juliet commented as she put on the headgear.

I spoke up, "Sorry we used them this morning."

Jane asked, "Do all of you do this?"

It was very apparent Jacob was a private person. We explained how everyone began with martial arts. I whispered to Juliet, "We need to show off Jacob's best skills." She agreed.

The three of us bowed to one another and began. Jacob lunged at me first. I provided him with punches and kicks he could easily block to show off his skills. Juliet did the same. He began throwing his kicks and punches. I blocked most of them, but let him get a few on me. I hit him gently a few times, though. We stopped and Jacob asked Greg and me to spar. Juliet took her gear off and gave it to Greg.

"Wait till you see these two go at it," Jacob said as he took his headgear off. "Juliet's superb too, but she's better with weapons."

Marty's face looked shocked. He asked, "Weapons? Did my son just say weapons?"

Juliet explained the differences in the styles of martial arts and how good she was with a pole. Greg and I began battling. We were not going easy on one another. I was using the same move I used on Eleni. I brought Greg to his knees when I wrapped my legs around his neck.

We had a great time. Jacob even showed his dad a few moves. We stayed there till nearly dinner time. It was nice getting to know more about Jacob and allowing his parents to get to know us and let them have a peek into Jacob's life. Juliet and I helped Jane clean up while the guys worked with Marty on the basics.

Jane had been putting the food in storage containers when she stopped and turned to Juliet and me. "Thank you. Jacob has always been a great kid. I've worried about him not having a lot of friends. Most of his friends are online and live all over the world. It's been nice to see him with you. I know Juliet and I have talked about this before. Since Jacob has been hanging out with the three of you, he has changed. He's more outgoing, doing better in school, and apparently is on his way to becoming a Kung-fu Master." She reached over and hugged us.

Once everything had cleaned up, Greg and I headed home for a quiet movie night at my house. We picked up pizza for everyone. At dinner, mom asked me to work on cleaning the attic after I was done with my exams. We discussed what kinds of treasure we might find up there. Everyone watched the Titanic movie with us. It was wonderful just hanging out with my mother. She works so hard. After the long day, I fell asleep soon after my head hit the pillow.

I woke up to my phone buzzing. Mechelle sent a group text about the dates of our trip. We only had a few weeks before our vacation. Before I went downstairs, I jumped in the shower. When I was drying off, I heard a noise in my bedroom. *What's ringing?* I looked at my phone with no missed calls. I heard it again. *Allison's phone.* I went to the drawer and saw several missed calls from her. Something must be up. She explained, "I need a personal favor. My best friend's son's in Iran. They captured him and were asking for weapons in exchange for his life. I have some surveillance pictures. I need you to get him. He's all she has."

I asked, "Are you crying?"

"Dyllons very dear to me. A fantastic kid," she said, trying to compose herself. "It needs to be done today. I'm going to leak information about him escaping and the direction he was heading. All you need to do is get him and take him to the location I give you. Special Forces can get him from there."

We worked out the details. I was going to arrive late at night. She texted me two pictures. The first was a camp, and the other was somewhere outside the camp. This would happen tonight. Greg and I discussed it. He was going with me. We did not know what condition he was in. I might need help with him. I had an idea to keep our secret from him. *Will it work?* I only hoped it would, but it required some shopping. Greg met me in the garage because my mother

144

thought we were out on a date. It would be midnight in Iran. I took him to my room and let him change into his outfit in my bathroom.

He came out and asked, "How do I look?"

"Heavenly," I commented. We looked in the full-length mirror at ourselves. "A man being held captive could easily believe we are angels."

"He better, or they are going to think he's crazy," Greg chuckled.

I looked at the photos again. I took the phone with me because Allison assured me it was untraceable. If there was a problem. I could easily let her know. The photo she sent showed a camp and there was an area marked where he was last seen.

We teleported to the area, making sure we were invisible while we searched for him. There were a lot of tents in rows. We were only a few feet from the area marked on the map. It was a hole in the ground. We looked down at it. The hole appeared to be just a little larger than the width of his shoulders. With telepathy, I asked Greg, "How are we going to get him out of there?"

"We need a rope," Greg said as he left to go find one. I stayed with Dyllon. He found one in the back of a vehicle a few yards away. While Greg tied the rope into a loop, he said, "I'm going to hold on to your ankles. You need to get the rope under his arms so I can pull him up."

I nodded to let him know I understood.

"Don't move," Greg instructed.

I turned my head to look in the direction he was looking. A man with a rifle was walking by. Once the coast was clear, Greg handed me the rope and motioned for me to go in. In the hole, I could not see a thing. There was also a potent smell of feces. What little moonlight I had was gone. It felt like he had enough room to lift one arm. I tapped him on the head. He moved a little.

"Greg, count to three and then move toward the tent behind you about 8 inches. Then lower me about six inches. I need to go into the earth to get the rope around him," I instructed. I was going up. "Stop. Something's wrong." *The necklace.* I was hanging upside down. The necklace was not touching me. I grabbed the necklace with my left hand. "Try again."

This was working, but I could only use my right hand. I felt around. Dyllon was next to me. I was able to get the rope around his head. It took some maneuvering, but I finally had the rope just below his fingertips. "Dyllon, you need to wake up. I need your help," I said, poking him in the stomach. He moved again. "If you can hear me, talk to me with your mind. Do not talk out loud. They'll hear you," I instructed.

He tried to move. "Mom, is that you?"

He was told to feel the rope and put it under his arms. I heard him moving. "Dyllon, is the rope under your arms?" I did not get an answer. Poked him again and repeated the question, while I tried to feel if I positioned it correctly.

"It's there," Dyllon informed me.

Greg asked, "How's it going?"

"Pull me up," I said excitedly.

I had to hold the necklace until I was completely out of the ground. We began pulling him up. It's working. Greg and I both pulled. We had to stop. Another man walked out of his tent and started smoking. Greg and I did all we could to hold Dyllon. The rope slipped a little. The man must not have heard it. Perhaps he was too far away. I looked into the hole. He was nearly high enough to reach.

"Hold the rope. I need to let go for a minute," I informed Greg. Quickly, I snatched the mirror from my bra and opened it and laid it down next to me. I had an idea. "Greg, we both need to pull with all our strength. If I can reach him, I can teleport him out of the hole. On three, I am going to let go of the rope and grab his hand. Do you understand?"

Greg nodded.

"Let's pull," I instructed. With all my strength, I pulled the rope. My hands were burning.

Greg pulled again on the rope. "He's almost at the top. Let's just pull him up," Greg advised.

I knew it would be easier to do it my way. He was high enough that I could easily reach him. I released one hand and grabbed his head. The rope slipped a little. I leaned back to make sure the stone was resting on my chest and looked in the mirror. I pictured us next to the tent, invisible.

Dyllon looked almost lifeless. Two men were approaching from the north. Dyllon moved. One man looked in our direction. Fortunately, we were all invisible. The man began looking around at the ground. He pulled a flashlight out and looked into the hole.

"He's escaped," the man screamed.

I grabbed the mirror and looked up. Men were coming from multiple directions. Greg grabbed me and Dyllon. I grabbed Dyllon and looked into the mirror, concentrating on the pickup location. Just as we were sucked in, I heard a gun fire.

We all collided as we hit the field. I looked around. We were all there. We made it!

"Brooke, look," Greg said, pointing to Dyllon. He was bleeding. They had shot him in the arm.

I grabbed him and the stone. It warmed. "Dyllon, you're going to be okay." As the wound was being healed, I noticed something popping out of his arm. It was the bullet.

"That's kinda cool," Greg stated.

Greg had the phone and handed it to me. I called Allison to let her know we were at the pickup location. The stone cooled. Dyllon opened his eyes and looked at us. "I think he may still be in shock. Dyllon, you were able to escape, and people are looking for you. You'll be safe soon," I told him. He grabbed my hand.

Greg started trying to clean the blood off his arm, but it just smeared it. Greg grabbed some dirt and rubbed it on his arm. It was less noticeable. "Brooke, we're visible," Greg informed me. I grabbed him and transported him back to Dyllon, invisible. I did not want to leave him.

We waited with him for about an hour when Allison called. "They should be there in ten minutes."

"Dyllon, ten minutes and you'll be safe," I told him. He looked around, but he could not see us.

Greg tapped me when he saw the serviceman. We backed away from Dyllon. They did not see him. "Greg, call out to them," I told him.

Greg said in a weak voice, "Over here." A light shined over Dyllon.

A voice in the dark said, "We got him." A man covered in camouflage came over to him. "I need a medic," he hollered.

I grabbed Greg's hand and teleported us back to my room. Greg looked at me and covered his mouth. His eyes were enormous. "What?"

He spun me around to face the full-length mirror. My once white outfit, along with the rest of me, was filthy. Greg went into the bathroom and changed out of his outfit and returned. I took him to my garage. He walked home from there. I returned to my bathroom for a much-needed shower.

I noticed Greg left Allison's phone on the bathroom counter. I called her to see how he was doing and to fill her in on the conditions he was in. She thanked us.

I had a hard time falling asleep that night because the condition of Dyllon and how they had him in the hole disturbed me. I was thankful he was safe.

Twenty-One

I thought the week would be worse with all the exams, but I was prepared, and they went smoothly. My last final was today. Immediately following it was my meeting with Mr. Thomas. I could not wait to see the final draft of my will. We reviewed the document before I signed it. *I'm adulting.* During our meeting, we discussed my summer trip. Mr. Thomas complimented me, "Lillie would be very proud of you." He paused for a moment and typed into his computer. "Your birthday is just around the corner. I sent your account a birthday present for your trip. Have fun."

I thanked him and took the copies of the will with me. When I was in my car, I checked my account. He had transferred a few hundred dollars to me. I wanted to celebrate the semester being over, but not everyone was done with their exams. I went to bed early to get started in the attic cleanup.

Phyllis made me an omelet for breakfast. She had errands to run and could not help me. I turned on the light. There really was not much light up there. I ran to the store and bought a couple of floor lamps, storage containers, and some shelving. Everything was scattered all over. The room did not have windows but could be converted into useful space. I got the boxes into the kitchen. At first, I wondered how I was going to get them to the third floor. I grabbed them and teleported us up there. *Another great use for the stone.* I cleared some space to put the shelving together. Once they were constructed, I looked around and created a space in the back of the room for everything we were going to keep. I would set things I came across that we had no use for near the door for Mom to check.

As I searched, I found some interesting items. There was a turntable and a record collection that I would love to move to the library. There was a great deal of items I was not interested in; a cuckoo clock, three pocket watches, a bunch of dolls, a postage stamp collection, and some really ugly furniture. They became part of the trash pile. I moved a small pile of antique rugs and dishes to the back of the room with some cool furniture. I found some keys in a box stuffed in the back of the attic. Two of the keys opened the trunks. The third one was unlocked. It contained a bunch of old clothes I could use as costumes if I needed them. The first trunk seemed to contain blankets. I figured I could use them when I move out. I pulled it away from the wall and dragged it to the back of the attic. When I returned, something in the wall caught my eye. There was an ammunition container hidden on the wall. I pulled it out. It contained some stacks of hundred-dollar bills and a piece of paper. The contents of this can go to my granddaughter Brooke. It was signed by Lillie Davis. They were fairly new. Grandma must have hidden this for emergencies. No one could have easily found it. I took it to my safe room in the villa and returned to cleaning the attic.

I had lost track of time. It was nearly 2:00 pm, and I had not eaten lunch. I grabbed something to eat and returned to the attic.

I returned to the trucks to explore the contents. The first locked trunk contained a note I could not read. It appeared to be a code of some sort. I sat back and let the stone touch me, and the code became a message.

Brooke,

If you have been able to decipher the message, you must have discovered the power of the stone and the unique gift you have inherited. In the house, we had a favorite place. There is a secret hidden within the house that not even Phyllis is aware of. Go to this place and find it's secret. Its secret will reveal much. Tell no one about it!

Love,

Lillie

What's she talking about? At this point, I did my work in the attic for the day. I began searching the house for our favorite place. I had fond memories of every room of this house. Every room but the attic. I searched for a bit, but I was tired. I took a shower and stopped wandering around the house, trying to find something I needed to put some thought into.

I spent the next few days cleaning the attic. Saturday, my mother came up to see what I had accomplished. She walked in and found a gigantic pile of things almost blocking the door. "Somehow this does not seem better," she commented.

I laughed, "That's the trash pile."

Mom looked through the pile. "I'm not sure about everything, but there are some valuable things in here. I need someone to tell me about the value of the other things," she informed me. Once she passed the pile, she noticed everything organized at the back of the attic. The Christmas items were on one shelf, dishes, and things on another, etc. "You have done an excellent job," Mom said before asking for the receipts for the things I purchased and told me she was going to pay me back.

The next few weeks passed quickly. Greg was helping on Austin's farm for extra cash for our trip and Jacob was interning at IBM. Juliet and I could spend a lot of time together. We hung out at her house mainly. She told me her mother suffered from depression. She didn't want to leave her alone. We still made time to go shopping for new bathing suits for our trip, trained together, got mani-pedis, and even hung out to cheer her up. I would go with Juliet when she would babysit. We planned fun activities for the kids to enjoy while we were there. My favorite was teaching them how to make homemade ice cream with orange soda and condensed milk. Juliet tried to give me some money to help, but I refused to take any.

It was nearly time for our trip. Mom had banned me from the third floor for weeks now. I think Mom had a gift for me up there. It must be too big to hide. I would be in South Carolina for my birthday, so my mother must plan to give it to me before I leave. Greg was too exhausted to hang out much, but tonight we have a date. He told me to wear something comfortable and casual, but not junky. I was specifically told no dresses. *What are you up to, Greg?* I could not figure out what he had in mind for me.

I dressed. I looked in the mirror, lifting my hair up. *Up or down?* I looked cuter with it down. *Down it is.* I grabbed a hair tie and tucked it into my pocket. I was spraying some perfume when there was a knock on my door. It was Mom.

She looked me over and asked, "Getting ready for your date?"

"Yes, Greg should be here in thirty minutes. He's taking me to dinner and then has a surprise for me," I explained.

Mom smiled, "How sweet. Do you mind staying up here until Greg gets here?"

Confused, I asked, "Sure, but what's up?"

"Say nothing, but you and Greg will eat here. You won't be here next week, and I wanted to make sure we celebrated your birthday. Phyllis has been cooking up something special for dinner. She wants it to be a surprise," she explained. Turning to leave, she pivoted back to me. "I'll send Greg up when she's ready for you to come down."

What's Phyllis up to? I slipped my shoes on and put the mirror in my pocket. I looked in the mirror to make sure I was ready to go. *Lip gloss.* I fiddled through a few to find the right shade. Once it was on; I was ready to go. I sat in the chair and scrolled through social media until Greg knocked on the door frame.

He smiled at me. "Are you ready?"

I stood up and took one last look in the mirror. "Yep." I grabbed his hand and headed downstairs. We were halfway down the flight of stairs when Greg asked me to close my eyes. He guided me down to ensure I did not fall. He turned me toward the sitting room and had me walk a few steps.

"Surprise!" I opened my eyes and saw my friends and a lot of balloons. Shocked by everyone I saw. I looked around the room to take in everyone. Jacob was with his parents, Juliet with her parents, Greg's parents and his sister, Austin and his sister, Lance, Gloria, Phyllis, and my mother. I walked around, thanking everyone for coming. My mother and Phyllis smiled in the archway to the dining room. "Phyllis cooking up something special, huh," I said to them. They both smiled at me and looked at one another.

"Your friends helped us with the guest list," Mom informed me.

"It's perfect. I love how you can meet the parents of my friends. They are great people. Make sure you spend time with them. You could use more friends," I said to my mother.

Mom announced, "Please help yourself to some food." She and Phyllis moved out of the doorway.

Gloria and I were in line together. "Thank you for coming," I said as I grabbed a plate.

"I'm glad Greg told me about it. I enjoy hanging out with you. They should have another jam next week," she informed me.

Disappointed I would not be there. I told her about my trip the following week. I looked over at the table. Phyllis had been busy. She had salad, pork tenderloin in a wine sauce, roasted cauliflower, mashed potatoes, brussel sprouts, and dinner rolls for us. Everyone was sitting all over the first floor. I sat with Juliet and her parents in the foyer. Mom had the dining room chairs arranged from the front door to just past the piano.

After dinner, Greg, Phyllis, and my mother collected everyone's plates and took them to the kitchen. The center of the table had my cake. Phyllis served my favorite Lemon cake with blueberries. It was fantastic.

I made my way around the room to make sure I conversed with everyone before the party ended. My mother had my presents on the bar in the sitting room. I opened my gifts and thanked everyone as I opened them. Greg got me the same set of protective gear we got Jacob for his birthday.

"There's one last gift, sweetheart. It's on the third floor if you would like to join us," my mother announced. "Greg, would you lead the way?"

It seemed like everyone followed us up to the third floor. Listening to the comments as I climbed the stairs, it seems they wanted to see more of our home. I heard Juliet explaining what was on the second floor to those around her. When we reached the landing on the third floor, Greg blindfolded me. He led me toward the attic. I heard the door open. He walked me in and took me across the room.

I heard my mother say, "No comments, please. Please head to that side of the room." I could hear footsteps on the hardwood floor.

I could not see a thing, but I felt a ceiling fan turn on.

Jacob asked, "Where do you want me to put this?"

"Do you mind holding it? I think she may need it soon," Mom said.

What am I going to need?

"Brooke, I could not be prouder of you. I suspect you moved here to be with me after Mom's death. I was so concerned about you leaving everything you've known. Your friends in Florida are amazing. I wasn't sure you would have relationships with people here. You have proven to me I worried for nothing." I could hear my mother struggling to hold back tears. "Brooke, you are flourishing. I look around this room and see the lives you have impacted in just a year," she chuckled. "A year ago, you would spend a few hours walking around the mall and would come home exhausted. Now... You're an athlete. I have watched your passion for martial arts grow. You astonish me," she sniffled.

As I listened to her talk, I felt my heart in my throat. Such kind words. Tears built up under the blindfold.

"With the help of Greg, Andrew, and Austin, my dream for you was realized," she said, choking up.

Greg took off the blindfold. I looked around the room. There were fully adjustable punching and kicking pads for training and mats on the floor. The room now had drywall and mom placed mirrors on two of the walls. Along the back wall was a cabinet holding a few towels. It had a small refrigerator on top of it. I looked at my mother and said, "What? Really, Mom?" I ran over to her and nearly tackled her when I gave her a hug. "Thank you." Tears were flowing down my face. I felt overwhelmed. Everyone started applauding.

"That's for you, sweetheart," my mother explained. She kissed me on the cheek.

I went over and thanked Austin, Andrew, and Greg. "Greg, you weren't helping Austin, were you?"

"No, but Bill has both of us for the summer once we get back from our trip," he said, wrapping his arms around me and kissing me on my forehead.

Juliet came over. "Your mother tasked me with keeping you away from the house while they worked on the room. You should know my mother is not really depressed." I gave her a big hug.

"Brooke, show us what you got," Gloria shouted.

Jacob brought me the gear Greg had given me. It felt awkward putting everything on while so many eyes were on me. I walked over to the training system and through a few strikes. I needed some practice to get a good rhythm going.

Greg tapped me on the shoulder. I swung around and nearly hit him. "You told me you would love for Austin to see how far you've come," Greg said as he stepped aside, revealing Austin wearing protective gear.

"Be nice," he said as he bowed to me.

"You better be careful, Austin. She's good," Andrew laughed.

I smiled with a crooked smile. I looked around the room. *Don't disappoint your fans.* I charged at him. He was able to block my punches. He threw a bunch. I leaned to the side, avoiding his swing and brought my leg behind his knee, bringing him to the ground. Everyone cheered. I reached down and helped Austin up.

"Impressive," he said, taking his headgear off.

On the way out of the room, a few people wanted to tour the home. Mom, Phyllis, and I took turns explaining the rooms and the history of the home. We hung out downstairs until everyone left. "Thank you for a wonderful party," I said to Phyllis and my mother.

We spent the rest of the evening cleaning up.

Twenty-Two

Mechelle was flying to her grandmother's house. Austin, Greg, and I rode together in Greg's truck. While Juliet and Jacob took Jacob's car. There would not be a vehicle for us to use while we were there because the six of us would not fit in one. We spent most of the ride enjoying the scenery and we played a game where we created a list of weird things to look for. Some items on the list were a pink elephant, a giant hammer, and a license plate for Hawaii. We never saw the license plate. With bathroom breaks, it took us over ten hours to get to Myrtle Beach. Mechelle asked us to make sure we arrived for dinner at 6:00 pm.

We pulled up to her grandmother's tan stilt home with white trim at 5:38 pm. The front of the home had stairs that led to a front porch the length of the house. There was a driveway that went under the home and was large enough to fit multiple cars. There was only one car parked under the home. They parked it to the right, near a door. Mechelle came on the porch and hollered, "Park both vehicles on the left side."

Greg pulled in under the house. He pulled up enough to allow Jacob to pull in behind him. To the right of the cars, just in front of the vehicle in the other parking spot, was the door. Mechelle emerged from it and about ran me over to give me a hug. She helped us carry up our luggage. We entered the home through the door in the parking area. The door led us to the kitchen where Mechelle's grandmother, Linda, was cooking. I dropped my bag and gave her a hug. The home smelled amazing. I knew we would have something incredible for dinner.

Linda pinched me on the cheek. "I've missed that beautiful smile."

Mechelle introduced her to everyone. I looked around. It was adorable. The ceilings had wood running from the kitchen into the living room.

"There are four bedrooms. My grandmother is in her room, but sadly, she's leaving tomorrow. I will move into her room once she leaves," Mechelle explained. "This way, ladies." She led us down to a room off of the living room. There was a twin bed and a full-size bed. "Juliet, you can have the twin bed. Brooke and I will share the full-size twin tonight." We dropped our suitcases and returned to the kitchen.

Mechelle escorted the guys to their rooms. They had a room like ours to choose from, or one with two twin beds. They decided one of them would have the room with the full-size bed to themselves. Linda told them they would need to figure that out after dinner.

The dining area was between the kitchen and the living room. We sat down and Linda asked Greg to say grace.

"Thank ya for the safe journey and this food. It looks amazing. In Jesus's name. Amen," Greg said nervously.

Linda said, "This is a Spanish-style chicken bake. I hope you enjoy it."

She baked everything in the same pan. There were onions, garlic cloves, chorizo, chicken thighs, and tomatoes with Spanish spices. While we ate, Linda led the conversation, "I want everyone to enjoy themselves while you're here. However, I have a few rules. First, girls sleep in their rooms and boys in theirs. There will be no hanky-panky." She lowered her head and looked at all of us over her glasses. "Second, please clean up after yourselves. I don't want bugs. The third rule could save a life. No swimming without a partner. The fourth and final rule is a deal-breaker. You must have a great time."

"Not a problem," Greg announced.

"Because I love my granddaughter. I have filled the refrigerator and the pantry with some of her favorite things. I hope you enjoy them. Please make yourself at home," she informed us. She went around the room and asked us questions to get to know us better until the meal was over. We cleared the table and carried everything to the kitchen. She kicked us out of the kitchen and told Mechelle to show us the beach. Just past some natural foliage was the ocean.

The back patio had a bench that ran along the banister. There were four rocking chairs, as well as a patio table that sat eight. We went downstairs and walked down the boardwalk between Linda's house and the next-door neighbor. It was a bit of a walk but as soon as Juliet, Mechelle, and I saw the beach, we took our shoes off and made and break for the shoreline. The guys slowly caught up to us. I looked up at them and noticed they seemed to take everything in. "None of you have been to a beach before?"

Austin had his mouth half-opened. He muttered, "It looks big on the television or in photos, but it doesn't do it justice. It's massive!"

"Massive is the best way to describe it," Greg added.

I watched their fascination with the ocean and remembered the day I saw snow for the first time. It was nearly dark, and the mosquitoes were biting. We grabbed our shoes and headed back to the house. At the bottom of the stairs, we found a towel hanging on a hook. Mechelle brushed the sand off her feet and handed the towel to me. Everyone repeated the process.

"This stuff really sticks," Austin announced.

Linda was wiping down the counters, "I know you're probably tired from the drive, but would anyone be interested in playing dominos?"

She was happy to teach us how to play chicken foot with the dominos. She and Mechelle were the only ones that knew the game. It was easy to learn, and we had a good time. We filled the house with laughter. When the game was over, Linda went to bed. She and her best friend were leaving for a cruise the next day. Mechelle put on the Avengers: Infinity War movie for us to watch. Many of us did not make it through the entire movie and headed to bed. I believe Juliet and Austin stayed up because during the night, Juliet told me to move over so she could get in the bed.

I woke up to a familiar smell. Someone was cooking Mexican scrambled eggs. At Mechelle's house, I have had them many times. I rolled over and noticed Mechelle was up. I woke Juliet, "We need to get up. Breakfast should be ready soon."

I changed and made my way to the kitchen. Mechelle was cracking eggs into a bowl and Linda was at the stove. Mechelle handed me some plates and asked me to set the table. Juliet emerged from our room.

Mechelle asked, "Juliet, please wake the guys?" Juliet knocked on the doors and announced it was time for breakfast while I finished setting the table. "There's American coffee in the pot," Mechelle announced. I got in line behind Mechelle for a cup.

159

Jacob and Austin came out in their pajamas. Linda looked them over. We sat down and had a wonderful meal. Linda reminded us again about the rules. Linda told us she needed to finish packing and asked us to do the dishes. Everyone pitched in. Jacob took the trash out for Linda. We hung out in the living room and dining room areas, trying to figure out what we wanted to do. We decided, after Linda leaves, to head to the beach. The guys were looking forward to swimming in the ocean.

We heard a horn honk out front. I followed Mechelle outside. There was a vehicle parked in front of the home. Mechelle held up a finger to let them know it would be a minute. She ran inside. I remained on the porch, sipping my second cup of coffee. I saw Mechelle take a suitcase from the vehicle. She must have been putting it in her grandmother's car. She walked over and began talking to the driver. About a minute later, Linda emerged and hugged her friends. I hollered down to her, "Have fun!" Linda waved back. They both hugged Mechelle and drove off in Linda's car.

Mechelle came up the stairs to the front porch. She instructed, "Let's get our bathing suits on." She grabbed my free hand and gently turned me around. We entered the home, and she announced, "The beach is now open." Everyone scattered to their rooms to change.

It was still a little early in the day for swimming. We made a giant sandcastle with a mote. Juliet showed her skills by adding windows to the building. The rays of the sun kissed my skin and warmed me up.

"Everyone lay in the sand at least six feet apart," Mechelle instructed. "I want to see your best sand angel!"

Everyone laid down and began moving their arms and legs. Mechelle pulled us up so we would not disturb our masterpieces. The guys started brushing the sand off. At least trying to. "Man, this stuff doesn't want to come off," Austin announced.

"You need a towel to get it all off or follow me," I said as I ran into the water. The waves were breaking against my body, throwing me backward. I finally dove under the crashing waves. Greg was still standing at the shoreline. Austin and Jacob joined him. Juliet grabbed Jacob's hand and dragged him in. He fell over when a gigantic wave ran into him.

Mechelle grabbed Austin's hand. They seemed to talk. They moved forward. Mechelle motioned for Greg to come with them. He did.

When Greg was past the break in the water, I swam to him. He kept looking in the water. I looked to see what he was looking at, but I saw nothing. I grabbed his hand and asked, "You, okay?"

With his eyes still fixed on the water, Greg asked, "Do you think there are sharks in here?"

I debated not telling him the truth. "Of course, there are." A look of shock appeared on his face. "Sweetie, In the past century or so there have only been about fifty shark attacks on public beaches. You have a better chance of being struck by lightning."

He asked, "It never occurred to me the last time we were at the beach, but the guys and I were talking about it last night. Are ya sure?"

"Yes," I assured him. The water was up to my chest. I wrapped my arms around his neck and kissed him. The swell lifted us up and brought us down with each wave. I looked around. Everyone was partnered off. Jacob and Juliet were kissing. I looked to the other side of me and found Mechelle with Austin. They were looking in the water. I jumped up and wrapped my legs around Greg's waist and kissed him again. Our eyes locked on one another. I inspected every inch of his face and began kissing the areas as I looked them over.

Greg looked me over as well and his eyes seemed to linger at my chest for a moment. He sunk me down in the water, covering me up to my shoulders, "We needed this. Things have been so hectic lately." He stood back up and lowered me down some. With one arm, he held me, and with the other, he ran across my neck. He gently pulled my neck to him and kissed me with passion.

Suddenly, we were being pelted with water from both sides. "Cool it down, you two," Austin yelled.

Greg and I smiled at one another while we tried to block the water with our hands. I tucked my face into his neck. Using telepathy, I said, "You get Austin and Mechelle. I'll get Jacob and Juliet. One, Two, Three." We both dove underwater and swam to our targets. I grabbed Jacob by the ankles and pulled him under. Juliet began dancing around, trying to avoid my grasp. She even tried climbing up Jacob once he recovered. I turned around and started kicking water at them. We had a good laugh.

Greg and Austin were rolling around, wrestling in the water. Greg came up for air and announced, "I'm done. I don't know how you hold your breath so long."

"Lots of years of practice at the lake, "Austin told him. He ran his hand over his hair, causing water to spray off. "I can hold it longer than most people."

Greg asked, "So, you think you can hold it longer than any of us?"

Austin looked around, "I don't see why not."

Greg looked at me. He smiled and asked, "Would anyone like to challenge Austin?"

"I'm pretty good," Juliet commented. "How about you, Brooke?"

I agreed and swam closer to them. "On my count," Greg announced.

"Wait, give me a minute. I need to warm up my lungs," Juliet said. Juliet held her breath for about thirty seconds and relaxed for a minute. She repeated the process. I tried to do this while she was doing it. Juliet nodded when she was done.

Greg counted us down. Austin lowered himself and tried to sit on the bottom of the ocean floor. I did the same as him. Juliet lay on the top of the water with her face looking down at us. The current was pushing me. It was a constant fight. Juliet and Greg periodically let a little air out of their lungs. I stopped fighting the current and let my body float to the surface. Juliet and I even knocked heads as I came up. I watched Austin struggle with the current. We had been under for a while. Greg went up to the surface, followed by Juliet. I knew the stone would permit me to stay under a lot longer, but I did not want it to seem so easy for me. I emerged acting like I need air.

"Dang, you gals are good." Austin complimented.

We had been on the beach for a few hours. Everyone agreed to head into town to have lunch. Austin and Juliet took their showers first. The girls were instructed to use Linda's bathroom while the guys used the guest bathroom. The rest of us hung out on the porch, waiting for our turn to bathe.

Mechelle asked, "While Austin's in the shower, would you mind telling me about some of your adventures?"

Juliet told her about us saving Kevin. She had played down her part in the story, but I made sure Mechelle had the full version of what happened. She asked Jacob about his role on the team. He told her about Anthony Granaldi nearly sitting on him while he was hacking his computer.

"Something I found interesting was when we had to find a secret room in Anthony's garage. Remember that Brooke," Greg said. He told Mechelle how the stone revealed the doorway. "It took us a few minutes to figure out how to open it."

The back door opened. Austin asked, "Who's next?"

Greg told Jacob to go next. Everyone began discussing what type of food to eat. Greg said something, and I thought about it. I needed to ask the stone to reveal the secret hidden in my house. I fought the urge to go there and find it, but I had all summer to figure it out. I wanted to enjoy a week just being me.

Over the next week, we had a great time. One of my favorites was a guided stand-up paddleboard tour. Everyone but Mechelle did well. Austin was so sweet the way he doted on her. She would fall off and he would help her get back on. I think it was probably her least favorite thing we did. Then again, she appeared to like the attention Austin gave her. Everyone enjoyed the sunset kayak tour. It was beautiful.

It was our last night there. Mechelle would stay here for another week. She planned on hanging out with her grandmother when she returned from her cruise. Tonight, was a date night. After showering, we picked out our outfits and made sure our makeup was perfect. We did not know what the guys had planned for us, but they told us to look nice. Each of us wore a sundress. Mine was denim. It had thin straps wrapped in front of me and tied to the side. Mechelle curled Juliet and my hair. We looked gorgeous!

There was a knock on the door. "Ladies, we need to get going," Greg announced.

As we walked out, it was easy to tell, it impressed them with how we looked. Greg gently caressed my bare shoulders. He whispered in my ear, "You look breathtaking." His breath on my neck sent chills down my body.

Jacob interrupted us because we were going to be late if we did not hurry. We pulled up to the Polynesian Fire Luau and Dinner Show. I was excited. I had always wanted to attend one of these. We enjoyed our meal before the show started. Our seats were right in front of the stage. Before the big performance, a performer asked our table to join them on the stage to learn the hula in front of the entire crowd. Before they showed us, they announced my birthday.

We lined up and listened and began following the instructor on what to do. Juliet already knew how to do this. They even asked her where she learned. Jacob and Austin seemed to struggle with the dance the most. It was quite humorous watching them.

Once we left the stage, the show began. There was a variety of entertainment. One man had flaming blades. He danced around the stage, providing a thrilling experience. My heart pounded as he and the other two performers danced with fire.

During the show, I thought I saw a man taking a wallet from a woman's purse. I watched him more closely to confirm. Many women had purses on the backs of their chairs. A man would bump into the women's chair, while another man took her wallet. They distracted the woman by the first man apologizing. Using telepathy, I filled Greg in on the situation and my plan and asked him to call the police. I told Juliet to follow me. The men appeared to be in their mid-twenties. I filled Juliet in and asked her to follow my lead.

Despite having zero alcohol in my system, I pretended to be drunk. I bumped into one man. He spun around to confront me. I said, "I'm so sorry. I didn't mean to run into you, but I'm glad I did. You're cute. I pretended to lose my balance.

Jacob and Greg walked past us and headed to the main entrance. I listened to them in my head. Jacob said they were going to greet the police and let them know who they were.

Juliet said, "He is cute, but your friend here is cuter." Her performance of a drunk person was perfect. Juliet tripped over my foot and fell toward the other man. He caught her and started flirting back with her. They wanted to buy us drinks, but I assured him we had enough. They tried to get us to leave the restaurant with them. Juliet told them she wanted to see the rest of the show.

In the corner of my eye, I noticed Jacob walk in with two officers. The two men had not noticed. They were too busy staring at our cleavage.

"I think these guys could show us a fantastic time. You guys lead the way, and we'll follow you out," I instructed. Their facial expressions said they were patting each other on the back. Juliet and I stayed back a little from them. They were saying something to one another and kept looking back to make sure we were still there.

One officer stopped them as they approached the door. They both turned in our direction and started taking off. Juliet and I both stood our ground in the aisle as they headed right for us, yelling, "Move!"

Juliet had one, and I had the other. Each of us with a powerful kick to the chest with a front kick. *Down you go...* I chuckled. The officers came over and handcuffed them. They asked us to follow

164

them out front. Everyone, including the performers, had their eyes on us and began applauding. We followed the officers to the front, where Jacob and Greg were waiting. After they patted them down and discovered many wallets. The officers placed them in the back of the police cars. The older officer took our statement while the other officer went into the restaurant. We were stuck here for a while. The officers needed to find the owners of the wallets and wanted to see if there were any more witnesses. They finally released us.

When we returned to the group, Austin said, "It was a nightmare trying to get the bills paid. What exactly happened?"

We filled him in on the way back home. Once the excitement of the evening calmed down, we went to bed because we had a long day of driving home in the morning.

Twenty-Three

We did not get home until nearly midnight because of a detour through Daniel Boone National Forest and a nice dinner in Lexington. I went to dress for my morning workout and noticed Phyllis had all my new workout clothes washed. I dressed before heading down to breakfast. Mom had already left for work. Phyllis had left me an apple cinnamon muffin and a note on the counter.

> Brooke,
>
> Sorry I could not join you for breakfast. I'm glad you're back. Enjoy the muffin. I won't be back until after dinner. There is lasagna in the refrigerator for dinner. The cooking directions are on the counter.
> Love,
> Phyllis

I grabbed the muffin and my coffee and headed to the back patio. The minute I walked outside, I heard birds chirping. When the weather was nice, I found it so relaxing sitting out there. I scrolled through the pictures of the last week and posted a few on social media. A picture Greg and I took together from the last Bloom Keeper's meeting became my new screen saver.

Once I finished my meal, I headed straight to my new training room. Normally I would run first, but I wanted to play with my new toys. I walked in and took in all my mother had done for me. It amazed me how talented Andrew and Greg were. Looking toward the sky, I said, "Thank you, Jesus." Feeling a bit overwhelmed with my blessings, I teared up. *God is so good to me.* I lifted my head and wiped my joyful tears and began stretching out. My phone chimed.

MOM:	I missed you, Peanut. I'm looking forward to hearing about your trip. See you at dinner.

I began punching and kicking the training pad. I got quite the workout. If I did not have the Bloom of Dreams, I would have a few bruises. The guilt of not running was getting to me. I ran for a few miles. I tried to create a list in my head of things I wanted to accomplish this summer. Let's see. *I need to read the new book in Audrey Rich's Stone Haven High Series, train more with Juliet, and I want to learn more about my grandmother's adventures.* I stopped dead in my tracks. *How could I forget? This house holds a secret for me.* I turned back and headed home. The more I thought about the secret, the more my mind raced. I picked up my pace. I nearly passed the gate at the front of our house as I tried to slow down.

Greg's truck was gone. He must have been at work already. I hurried up the walk. In my excitement, I had a difficult time getting the key into the lock. I went to the kitchen for water. As the sweat dripped off me, I grabbed a kitchen towel and headed to my shower before starting my search.

I reached for my hair dryer. Nope, not today. My mind focused on my next mission, finding out about the secret. I twisted my hair up and clipped it. I grabbed the note from my drawer and read it again. Think about our favorite spot in the house. The spot we spent many hours together. *That could be anywhere.* It only made sense to start on the second floor because I was already there. I asked the stone to reveal secret passages. I looked around my room and found nothing. My bathroom revealed nothing.

The balcony? Grandma and I never really spent much time there. I did though. Curious, I checked. *Would you look at that?* A brick was lit up. I removed the brick, which revealed a small compartment with a key. I took the key and examined it. It was not like the iron keys for the doors in the house. It was a modern key. I put the key in my pocket. My search continued in Phyllis's room. Her room revealed nothing, the spare room had nothing either. *Up or down?* I contemplated the direction to go. *Up it is!* I headed up to the third floor. There was nothing in the guest room. However, Mom's room fireplace was another story. One brick revealed a secret compartment. It was empty. I sat on her bed, a little disappointed I did not find another treasure. My new room and the storage room showed nothing. I used the mirror in my training room to teleport down to the kitchen pantry.

One shelf lit up. I pulled on it. It seemed to be on a hinge and revealed a small, safe room. It did not look like a place anyone could stay for long. Two people would fit comfortably. Grandma, you have a lot of secrets. I closed the door and continued looking. The kitchen had a surprise. Phyllis baked a Kentucky Derby pie, but no secret hid in it. The laundry room and mud room were also duds. I exited the kitchen and headed down the hall. *The piano would be a great place to hide something.* Again, nothing. I sighed. I was getting discouraged. The dining room and sitting room revealed fresh flowers, but nothing else. I looked around the front door and the desk. Nothing.

I sat down at the desk. *What am I missing?* I ran the floor plan through my head. *The garage?* It couldn't be there. The only time we spent time there was getting in and out of the car. I looked down at the stone and said, "Show me something." Nothing happened.

My phone started ringing. I looked down. It was Greg. "Hey honey," I said.

Greg said, "I need a favor. Dad called me. He said Mom's doctor told them it looked like there might be more cancer. He is sending her for a test. She wants us to pray over her tonight. The pastor is even coming over. Can ya do your thing tonight?"

"Yes. She'll need to be asleep," I informed him. "What time do you want me to come over?"

Greg said, "Dad is telling everyone to come at 7:30. I would say midnight for our next mission."

"I'll see you at 7:30. I love you," I said. It hurt me to know his family was suffering, but tonight her prayers will be answered. I said a prayer for her. *Thanked God for the ability to heal her.*

Back to the current mission. I looked around. I asked the stone to show me again. Nothing. *What am I missing? What would Grandma say?* I closed my eyes and thought. *She would pray. Mom would too.* "Father God, in the name of Jesus, thank you for guiding me and being with me with all that I do. Lord, I'm lost. Please help me remember where my grandmother's favorite spot with me was. Amen," I prayed.

My gut began telling me to go upstairs. I've checked everywhere up there. Rather than fight the nagging feeling, which I knew was God, I headed upstairs. I was seeing nothing. I walked around the landing. My gut was telling me to go downstairs. I was getting frustrated. The bench was halfway down the stairs. I sat down. *What is the stone trying to tell me?* I thought about what we did together. We did crafts in the dining room. She and I planted things in the garden. *Could it be outside? What else?* I would pick a book from the lower shelf in the library. That's where she kept books I would like. We would read them together. *Wait... We sat here for hours, reading. We sat here reading all the time!* I stood up and looked around the bench, but I saw nothing. *I can't believe I forgot.*

I held the stone and said, "Reveal any secret doors." The bench began glowing. I moved the pillows and felt around. I pulled and pushed on the panels. Nothing was happening. It occurred to me someone could accidentally push a button or something to open it if it was on the seat. Just past the seat, I ran my hand on the panel and found nothing. Moving down past the seating area, I pushed and ran my fingers along the wood. I gently pushed on the top strip of wood along the wall. There was a small piece of wood that was about an inch long. I pushed down on it. The paneling opened and the right side of the seat lifted a little, revealing a narrow steep stairway heading down. It was very dark inside.

I heard what sounded like the back door. *Oh no. How do I close it?* I pushed the button nothing happened. It suddenly closed on its own. *It must be on a timer or something.*

Mom called out to me, "Brooke! Are you down here?"

I put the pillows back on the bench and went downstairs. "You're home early." We hugged each other.

"I missed you. I thought we could have a pleasant night with just the two of us," Mom explained.

"That's a great idea. Only Greg asked us to come over tonight to pray for Joann. She's not improving as they would like. They want us over at 7:30 pm," I informed her.

"We still have plenty of time before then to hang out," I said, as I put the lasagna in the oven. How about a movie while we wait?"

As we walked up to the library, the secret passage I found tormented me. I needed to know what was down there. We went to the library and put on our favorite movie, Pride and Prejudice. I can't tell you how many times we have seen this movie. We had many of the lines memorized and occasionally we would say the character's lines. Mom and I snuggled up together, enjoying the movie until the lasagna was done. We ate in the kitchen. I took that time to tell her about my trip and show her pictures of everything we did. It was so nice hanging out. We had a fantastic time. We did the dishes and

170

returned to our movie. I had set an alarm on my phone to remind us to head over to Greg's house. The movie took my mind off the secret passage. I was laying with my head in my mother's lap when the alarm went off. We paused the movie and headed over to Greg's house.

The pastor was already there when we arrived. "Thank you for coming," Andrew said as he let us in. We followed him to the dining room.

Joann gave mom and me a hug and introduced us to the pastor. Mom and Joann caught up on what had been going on since they last saw one another. Joann explained and thanked us for coming. Everyone sat around the table holding hands while the pastor led us in prayer for healing. Out of fear the stone might begin to warm, I leaned forward to make sure it was not touching my skin. When the prayer was over, the pastor hung around for a few minutes before he left. Mom and Joann were enjoying their conversation. Greg and I headed out to the patio.

We confirmed our plans to heal his mother. I would meet him in his room. Karen came out and joined us. She asked me, "Do you think we could do something together over the summer?"

I replied, "I would love to. What do you have in mind?"

She gave me a long list of things.

My mother interrupted our conversation. She said, "Time to go."

I kissed Greg and gave Karen a hug before leaving.

Mom and I put on our pajamas and returned to our movie. It was late when it ended. Mom came in and tucked me in. She had not done that in years. We chatted for a while. She kissed me on the head and headed upstairs. I was nearly asleep when I realized I needed to set an alarm. Before dozing off, I set the alarm on my phone. I did not miss meeting Greg.

My alarm went off. I popped into Greg's bedroom. He was sitting on his bed waiting for me. He stood up and handed me his phone, showing me a picture. Greg said, "I took a picture of their bedroom. They keep the door shut, and Dad is a light sleeper, so make sure you're quiet."

I grabbed his arm and teleported us to her room. I took the Bloom of Dreams off and handed it to Greg. He looked at me, confused. I grabbed the stone and, using telepathy, I said, "You should heal her." His eyes began to tear up. "Hold it in one hand and touch her with the other. Ask the stone to heal her."

Greg placed his hand gently on Joann's hand. He closed his eyes. "If the stone cools down, it's done healing," I whispered.

He continued, holding her hand a little longer. I felt tears filling up for him. I was thankful she could be healed. He handed me back the stone. I held it in my hand and teleported us back to his room. Greg pulled me in and hugged me. "Thank you," he whispered in my ear.

"You're welcome. She'll be fine now," I need to get to bed. I kissed him good night.

I returned home and crashed immediately.

I awoke at 7:45 am when Greg's call. He said enthusiastically, "Mom was up early this morning. She fixed us breakfast and said she felt fabulous. Mom believes God healed her. The scar from her surgery is gone. She's completely healed."

"That's wonderful news," I told him in a groggy voice.

"I'm sorry for waking ya, but I couldn't wait to tell ya. Thanks again for letting me heal her," Greg said, sounding emotional. "It was a great honor to be able to do that. I know now how you feel doing all the amazing things you can do. I gotta go. Bill wants me to repair some fences. Love ya."

I thought about going back to sleep, but my thoughts were on finding out more about my grandmother's secret. This motivated me to get dressed and head downstairs for breakfast.

"You're up early. You just missed your mother," Phyllis said, as she read her paper. I grabbed a cup of coffee and a yogurt from the refrigerator. I joined her in the dining room. "Do you want me to fix you something?"

I ripped the top off the yogurt. "No. This will be fine. If I need more, I'll grab a piece of fruit later," I told her. I filled her in about us praying over Joann and Greg healing her.

"That was nice of you, but remember, you can't heal everyone. It's risky. Someone could connect the healing to you. Especially those aware the stone has powers. Many do not know all the power it possesses; you may not even know all it can do. Those interested in it are watching and the more they know, the more danger you are in," Phyllis warned.

I blew on my coffee to cool it off. "I understand. What are you doing today?"

Phyllis laid her paper on the table. She asked, "I need to run some errands. Would you like to join me?"

"Another time. I'm still recuperating from my trip." I scraped the last of my yogurt from the cup.

"It looks like you are peeling," she commented.

"I sure am," I said, showed her my shoulder, which was still very red. "When are you headed out?"

"As soon as I finish my coffee," she said, taking another sip.

"Don't worry if you can't find me. I might be in and out today." After grabbing the trash from the patio table, I headed back to the kitchen. I loaded my cup into the dishwasher and headed to my room.

I grabbed a flashlight from my side table and waited for Phyllis to leave before opening the stairwell again. The secret entrance did not stay open long. I turned on the flashlight and headed down the narrow passage. At the opening, the ceiling was low. *This place is creepy.* I slowly made my way down, not knowing what to expect at the bottom. My heart was racing. A short hallway with one door was at the end of the stairwell. I reached for the handle and noticed my hand shaking. *Brooke, you're being silly. No one has been down here but Grandma.* I grabbed the door handle. Locked. I knew I could just walk through the door, but I remembered the key I had found.

I pulled out the mirror and retrieved the key I had forgotten about from my pants pocket and returned to the hallway. The key opened the door. The lights in the room immediately came on, revealing what appeared to be my grandmother's special operations room. There were maps along one wall with marker pens in it. Grandma had attached small labels to the pens.

An antique 21-drawer apothecary filing cabinet made of wood was on the same wall, along with a bookshelf. Two wardrobe cabinets were on one wall. Opposite that wall was a large Oak antique desk with a laptop computer, lamp, and a printer on top of it. The desk contained a small notepad and pencil, scissors, flashlight, pens, and files. Next to the desk was a cabinet with a microscope on top of it. The cabinet contained a gun, bottles with pills, night vision monocular, surveillance equipment, ropes, and zip ties. There was even a mobile phone jammer. Or at least that is what one looks like in the movies. There was something that looked like it went to a computer. I would need to ask Jacob about it. There was a device that looked like one of those spy things in a movie that amplified the sound. There were many other things I was not sure what they were for. All these things seemed so useful.

173

I opened one wardrobe. It had a variety of clothes. Everything from riding outfits to formal gowns. We were about the same size. These could be useful. One side had shoes on a shelf. Along the door were a variety of jewelry choices. The other wardrobe contained wigs, hats, and surveillance outfits.

The bookshelf contained what looked like a bunch of journals. A few of the books were flipped backward. I pulled one of them out. It was empty. I grabbed another with its spine facing out. It was a journal and appeared to be my grandmother's handwriting. Dates were at the top of the pages. I put that one back and grabbed the one next to the blank ones. It was partially filled out. The last entry read.

May 14

Imelda, Anthony Granaldi III's cousin, contacted me. She knows he is evil. Imelda suspects her son is dead because of him. She provided me with blueprints of his home. She overheard him talking to his wife about a secret room in Anthony's house. I started searching for the room.

Marshall may have figured out where I live. I've warned Phyllis to keep an eye out for any strangers lurking around. I'll be heading to France to see what I can find out about him.

I'm looking forward to passing the Bloom on to Brooke. She will be 18 soon. I plan to take her to Italy to meet Isabella and Leonardo. She must rely on them. They will assist her with anything she needs. Brooke will be shocked to find out she will inherit millions. We'll need to travel to Japan to connect with Asahi Abe. Her training will begin with him immediately. She will only have a few months before college starts to train with him.

I finally had a lead on who may have killed her. Marshall Blaise, I'll be paying you a visit. The urge to read all about all my grandmother's adventures would need to wait. I felt it was important to document my adventures for the past year before I forget them. There was plenty of time to read the journals and learn more about my grandmother.

Let's see, where do I begin…

Discover other titles by D.A. Dwinell

Guardian of the Stone Series
The Bloom of Dreams – Book 1
The Bloom's Cradle - Book 2
Bloom Keepers - Book 3
Path of the Guardian – Book 4

Connect with D.A. Dwinell
If you want the latest news on D.A. Dwinell or interested in connecting on social media, please visit the following site:
www.facebook.com/DADwinell
Instagram: d.a._dwinell